A

BAD

NIGHT'S

SLEEP

A

BAD

NIGHT'S

SLEEP

MICHAEL

WILEY

MINOTAUR BOOKS

A THOMAS DUNNE BOOK
NEW YORK

This is a work of fiction. All of the characters, organizations, and events portrayed in this novel are either products of the author's imagination or are used fictitiously.

A THOMAS DUNNE BOOK FOR MINOTAUR BOOKS.
An imprint of St. Martin's Publishing Group.

www.thomasdunnebooks.com
www.minotaurbooks.com

Library of Congress Cataloging-in-Publication Data

Wiley, Michael, 1961–
    A bad night's sleep : a mystery / Michael Wiley. — 1st ed.
        p. cm.
    "A Thomas Dunne book."
    ISBN 978-0-312-55224-4
    1. Private investigators—Illinois—Chicago—Fiction.   2. Police corruption—Illinois—Chicago—Fiction.   3. Undercover operations—Fiction.   4. Chicago (Ill.)—Fiction.   I. Title.
    PS3623.I5433B34 2011
    813'.6—dc22

                                                    2011005107

First Edition: June 2011

10 9 8 7 6 5 4 3 2 1

To my family, near and far

ACKNOWLEDGMENTS

Thank you to Julie and Sam, for reading, rereading, and advising; George and Sally, for teaching me more than a few things along the way; Dave, for making me look better in lights than I might otherwise look; Isaac, Maya, and Elias, for keeping me laughing; Philip and Lukas, for representing and advocating for this, that, and everything better than anyone else; and Toni and Ruth, for making everything right.

A

BAD

NIGHT'S

SLEEP

Fifteen Illinois law enforcement officers were charged Tuesday in an FBI sting on counts that included accepting cash in exchange for providing armed protection for drug dealing operations in south suburban Chicago.

—The New York Times

ONE

THE SOUTHSHORE CORPORATION OWNED a seven-block chunk of land on the south side of Chicago. If they'd let it sit for twenty years, it would have turned back into the prairie that had stood there a couple of centuries ago. Thirty years and you could've put on a coonskin hat and gone deer hunting. But the Southshore Corporation hadn't let the land sit. Two weeks after the owners signed the final contracts, workers had poured the foundations for a mix of single-unit houses and condo blocks that the corporation was advertising as Southshore Village. The corporation promised to build a small town in the middle of the city. The brochures included a picture of kids playing baseball on a cul-de-sac and another of a middle-aged man and woman sitting on a porch swing. The faces were black, white, brown, and yellow. It was a pretty dream and the Southshore Corporation had the money to make it come true.

I sat in my car on the construction site on a cold November night. The street was packed dirt and clay. Bare bulbs hung from wires strung from poles but the place was mostly dark.

Ripped plastic sheets blew through the open windows on the buildings. Three A.M. had come and gone. I cranked the heater and the warm air made me sleepy. I flipped the heater off. Above, the moon shined dully through a thin layer of clouds.

The thefts had started right after the Southshore Corporation began putting up buildings. Tools and building materials disappeared first, then appliances and construction equipment. The corporation had strung a wire-link fence around the site, put up security cameras, and paid for extra police patrols, but the thefts had continued. One night the thieves stole the security cameras. Another, they took thirty thousand dollars' worth of copper wire from a storage trailer.

Jen Horlarche, the corporate vice president in charge of development, had hired me to camp out at the site and stop the thefts. I figured I would do no better than the security cameras and police patrols and I told her so. I also said, "I don't do security, not even glamorized."

She said, "There's nothing glamorous about this job."

I looked at her eyes and her smile and said, "I find that hard to believe. Besides, I've seen the Southshore brochure."

"You don't get to spend time with me," she said, "and the place won't look like the brochure for another fourteen months—longer if the thefts don't stop."

I said, "I've got a seventeen-year-old Buick Skylark with a heater that still works. If that interests you."

Her smile fell but her eyes still made me think I would like to get to know her better, so I let her write me a check and I put it in the bank and now I sat alone in my cold Skylark, waiting and watching.

When I started to drift to sleep, I shifted into drive and

bounced over the dirt until I found an almost completed house with an open garage on a street that dead-ended into three storage trailers. I backed my car into the garage and peered into the night like an animal snug in its burrow. I closed my eyes. Opened them. Closed them.

A car engine woke me, and tires grinding over the dirt and clay. It was still dark. The car neared and I slid low in my seat, wondering if my Skylark was visible from outside. The car slowed and stopped next to the storage trailers.

I laughed. It was a police cruiser making its rounds.

Two cops sat in the car. The driver got out and went to the trailers, rattled the padlocked doors. They were secure. He walked back to the cruiser, pulled out a cell phone, and talked into it for awhile. He hung up and got into the car. The cops sat some more. The night was quiet. They were in no rush.

The other cop got out and went to the trunk, opened it. He removed a pair of bolt cutters and looked up and down the street. He went to the closest trailer.

"Don't do it," I mumbled.

He did it. The lock fell to the ground and he swung the trailer door open. Then he went to the other trailers.

His partner got out of the car with a flashlight. He shined it everywhere but at me. He went to the first trailer and looked inside.

More engines approached. More tires rolled over the dirt and clay. Three dark vans pulled behind the patrol car and guys in jeans and jackets climbed out of each. They shook hands with the cops and went to the first trailer. They rolled large spools of wire out of the first and loaded them into the vans.

I fished my cell phone from my jacket. I punched in the

number Jen Horlarche gave me when she hired me. Her home number. "Just in case," she'd said with that smile. It was 3:30 in the morning but this was a just-in-case moment.

She answered the phone on the second ring. A light sleeper. "Yeah?"

I told her who was calling, explained the situation, and asked, "What do you want me to do?"

"Call the police." Like it was obvious.

"The police are already here."

"Call the *other* police," she said.

"With cops involved on both sides, it'll be messy," I said. "No one will be happy about this coming into the open."

She thought about that for a moment. "Call them," she said.

I dialed 911. The operator sounded doubtful when I told him what was happening. His supervisor sounded doubtful when I explained again. "No sirens or lights," I said, "and if you put this on the radio, they'll be gone before you get here."

The supervisor said, "You're telling me to send officers into a situation without radio contact?"

I knew she was worried I was setting up a trap. "Yeah," I said. "You use the radio and they'll hear you."

She asked for my name and identification.

"They're moving to the second trailer," I said. They were unloading more spools of wire. Southshore Village was going to go without electricity.

"Name and ID," she said, like we had all the time in the world.

"Joe Kozmarski," I said and gave her the nine digits on my private detective's license.

She never told me if the police were coming without radio but eight minutes later four squad cars rolled around the corner onto the dead-end street. The two lead cars flipped on spotlights and the cold night went brilliant.

The men at the trailer froze.

The four squad cars stopped. A car-mounted bullhorn told the men to raise their hands and step forward into the light.

The uniformed patrolman who'd snipped the locks off the trailers took five steps toward the squad cars, his hands in the air. He moved slow, like he was walking into a fire, but he did as he was told.

The others stayed frozen. Four of them. That meant three more, including the other patrolman, were hiding in the trailers.

The squad cars rolled closer. The bullhorn crackled and told the men again to raise their hands. The amplified voice sounded frightened.

Two of the thieves ran, one onto the dirt lot behind the trailers, one toward a van. The others stayed where they were.

The officers jumped out of their cars, drew their weapons, yelled at the thieves to stop.

The one on the dirt lot kept running. The one who'd run to the van climbed in and started the engine. The one in uniform who'd stepped forward when he was told to lowered his hands and took his service pistol from its holster. A gunshot exploded—not from his gun. Everyone froze, even the thief on the dirt lot. All was silent except for the hum of car engines.

I switched the dome light all the way off in my Skylark, took my Glock from its holster, opened the door, and slipped out into the garage.

A tall cop, who seemed to be in charge, yelled at the thieves, "Put your guns down!"

The one in uniform stooped and laid his gun on the dirt, stood with his hands in the air. He was shaking.

Another gunshot exploded and the tall cop went down. A cop screamed, "Fuck!" and opened fire. Then everyone was shooting. The uniformed thief who'd just laid his gun on the ground took a bullet in his head, flew back, and landed in the dirt. The thief on the dirt lot sprinted toward a Dumpster. Some of the others followed him. The van spun its tires in the dirt and headed toward the police. A gunshot from a crouching officer blasted its windshield. The van slid, turned, headed back toward the trailers, and bounced over the open lot. Then it slowed, the passenger door opened, and the thieves who'd run onto the lot climbed in.

The three men who were still hiding in trailers—the other uniformed thief and his friends—poured out and ran. The one in uniform ran to a van and hid behind it. He was twenty yards from me, no more. His friends ran to another van, got in through the back, started it, cut a hard circle. A hand holding a pistol stuck out of the passenger-side window. The pistol aimed at an officer who was shouting into a handheld radio and fired. The officer stopped shouting and fell face forward into the dirt. The van bounced away over the open lot.

The only thief who remained was the patrolman hiding behind the van. He must've known there was no way out. Bullets had blown out the tires under his patrol car and shattered the lights on top. His partner had a slug in his head. He couldn't drive away in the van and pretend he hadn't been on the scene. He was already worse than dead. At most, he could delay the officers and help his partners get away.

He raised his gun over the hood of the van.

The cops huddling behind their squad cars fired at him—

fifty shots, a hundred, more, a wall of noise. He ducked back and the shots sank into the dirt and into the side of the van.

I aimed my Glock at him. It was an easy shot. But I couldn't take it. I'd been a cop until my bad habits had gotten me fired. My dad had been a cop. A good one.

Everything got quiet.

The officer who'd gotten shot while shouting into his radio pushed himself onto his elbows and crawled toward the squad cars. The other officers saw him. One of them ran to help.

The man hiding behind the van raised his gun over the hood and aimed at them. I shook my head, sadder than I'd ever been before. I squeezed the trigger and felt my Glock bolt against my palm as it fired.

I heard nothing.

I saw nothing.

I knew that I'd shot a thief who was aiming his gun at two officers, but I also knew that the thief was wearing a police uniform. I stumbled back to my Skylark, sat in the front seat, and closed my eyes.

TWO

A TREMBLING COP HANDCUFFED me, took my gun and ID, and shoved me to the ground. I stayed where I landed, my cheek to the cold dirt, like a hunter's kill trussed and ready to be strapped to the hood. If I stood and ran, if I moved, if I even twitched, the cop would shoot me. He told me he would. I said nothing. I didn't move. I kept my cheek to the dirt.

For a long time they left me there. Like a dead animal. Cops ran across the lot, yelled at each other, peered into empty buildings with flashlights. Someone was sobbing. Sirens howled on all sides, far and near. Five men had taken bullets. Six ambulances pulled into the street. You get little extras like that if you wear a uniform, even if you're a thief. Police helicopters scoured the ground with searchlights. News helicopters flew above them.

Two men and a woman approached. They were cops too. The men wore jeans and heavy jackets. The woman wore gray slacks and a leather coat. The men grabbed my arms and hoisted me to my feet. The woman gritted her teeth and looked me in the eyes. She brushed the dirt off my face with the back of her hand. Not gently. Like the dirt annoyed her and she thought it ran deep into my skin. She nodded toward an unmarked sedan, and the men steered me to it.

The men got into the backseat with me, one on each side. The woman got into the front. Like the cop who handcuffed me, she trembled, but with anger. "Okay, Mr. Kozmarski," she said, "what happened here?" Her eyes had fire in them. I figured mine did too. I looked out the window into the floodlit cold. An hour had passed since the shooting stopped, maybe more, but cops darted from building to building, car to car, like they were running for cover. The night had gone bad and looked like it was getting worse. "Mr. Kozmarski?" the woman said.

My lawyer, Larry Weiss, who usually got me out of jams, would've told me to keep my mouth shut. I didn't care. I gave it all to her. Jen Horlarche hiring me to secure the Southshore Village property. Me drifting to sleep in the garage. Two cops breaking into the construction trailers. Six men arriving in vans and stealing spools of copper wire. The chaos that followed. Me drawing a bead on the thief-cop, hesitating until he pointed his gun at other cops, then pulling the trigger. "Is he dead?" I asked when I finished.

"He died on the way to the hospital."

"Damn," I said. I figured that the partner of the man I shot—the one who'd tried to surrender when the squad cars arrived—was dead too. You don't take a bullet in the forehead and survive. "The others?" I said.

"One critical, two stable." She turned away as though looking at me disgusted her. She lit a cigarette, threw the lighted match out of the window.

The first light of morning was graying the night sky. Soon

the sun would rise and dry the pools of blood. Or else a cold rain would wash the blood into the dirt. Then kids would play baseball on the dead-end street and a middle-aged couple would sit on a porch swing at the house where I'd hidden in the garage and watched as the shooting started.

In the front seat of the sedan, the woman cop pulled my wallet from her coat pocket. She leafed through the cash and pulled the credit cards and ID from their slots. She read them like she was going to tell my fortune. She looked at my detective's license. "Says you're a PI since 1998. What did you do before then?"

I swallowed. "I was a cop."

She laughed. It wasn't a nice laugh. "Let me guess. They fired you."

I shrugged. "Something like that."

The man on my right said, "Let's hear it."

I said nothing.

The other man said, "It's on file. You can tell it or we can read it."

I shrugged again. "I was drunk and high and crashed my cruiser into a newsstand."

I wished they would laugh. The woman cop nodded like she'd expected as much. The man on my right said, "Were you high tonight, Mr. Kozmarski?"

If the handcuffs hadn't been chafing my wrists, I would have hit him. I said, "I've been clean for seven years."

"I want a toxicology test," the woman said to him. She threw my wallet at my chest. It bounced to the floor.

"Do I get my gun?" I said.

"Yeah, I'll throw that at you too." She looked me in the eyes. "No, you don't get your gun. It's impounded. Maybe in a year, if you're lucky, you'll see it. If ballistics shows that you shot more than the one round that you admit to, or if that round turns up in an unexpected body, you'll never see it again. Won't matter, though—you'll be in jail or strapped to a gurney waiting for an injection."

"You're arresting me?"

She shook her head. "I'm taking you in as a material witness."

"You'll need a judge to keep me."

"Five officers have bullets in them. You think the judge will refuse me?"

"More would've been shot if I hadn't done what I did."

"A couple of them might be driving to the department right now instead of lying in the back of an ambulance if you'd done something sooner."

I had nothing to say to that.

They took me to the 1st District Police Station on South State Street. It was a two-story gray concrete fortress with little windows—bigger than gun turrets but nothing to squeeze through if you weighed more than eighty pounds. Television news vans lined the curb in front, and a crowd of thirty or forty reporters with cameras and microphones surrounded a man whose head rose above them. The man was in a dress uniform.

"Shit," said the woman cop in the front seat.

At the corner a concession truck advertised donuts, bagels, and hot coffee. No one was buying. Even the guy in the truck was leaning toward the crowd listening for details about blood and death. I could have told him the details were nothing he wanted to hear but he wouldn't have paid attention to me. The unmarked car we were in swung past him onto 17th Street. A block to the west a hundred police cruisers stood in a parking lot, empty, engines cold, like the city knew nothing but peace. Before we reached them the unmarked car turned into a driveway that led to a side door into the station.

INSIDE, A ROW OF chairs was bolted to the floor and wall. The woman cop told me to sit and one of the men unlocked my handcuffs, then relocked my left wrist to a metal bar. The woman cop said, "Make yourself comfortable," and the three of them went through a glass office door. The hallway smelled like sweat and ammonia. Guys who'd sat in the chairs before me had scratched gang graffiti into the plastic. I wanted to scratch *Help!* but figured anyone who ended up on these chairs couldn't do me much good.

I fished my phone from my pocket and dialed Larry Weiss's home number. He worked late and then played cards most nights, usually arriving at his law office between ten and eleven A.M. He would schedule meetings at midnight and had bailed me out more than once at two in the morning without complaining, but he considered calls at dawn an insult.

His wife answered the phone and handed it to Larry.

"What?" he said.

"Hey," I said, "it's Joe."

"I'm not a fucking banker," he said. "Call me later." He hung up.

I dialed again.

The phone rang twice and he picked up. "What?" He stretched the word, made it sound like the phone was hurting him.

I gave him a short version of the night.

When I finished, he said, "Holy shit, Joe." The words of a professional.

"Yeah," I said.

"Don't say anything to anyone," he said. "Not till I'm sitting by your side." He paused. "But you know that already."

"Yeah, I do."

"They can hold you for twenty-four hours. Forty-eight, tops."

"They should be shaking my hand and pinning ribbons on my shirt. I ended the situation before anyone else got hurt."

"Yeah, but you shot a cop."

"A thief."

"A thief in a uniform."

"Yeah," I admitted. "How soon can you be here?"

"I'm stepping into the shower right now. Give me an hour."

"Thanks, Larry. I'm counting on you."

He let that sit for a moment, said, "Joe?"

"Yeah?"

"You might want a real lawyer on this."

"You're real enough for me."

"I mean someone good."

"You've always done the job right," I said.

"I'm just saying. Dead cops and all. Someone's gotta fall. I don't want it to be you."

"I appreciate that, Larry."

"Keep your head together."

"It's never been together," I said. "Why should it be now?"

We hung up.

Voices came from behind the door where the woman cop and her partners had disappeared.

I cupped the phone in my palm.

The voices faded.

I dialed my ex-wife Corrine at the landscaping business she ran from a storefront on the Northside. She was there most mornings before the sun rose.

She had caller ID and she answered, frightened, "What the hell is happening?"

Two years after the divorce we were working at getting back together. But every time we got close I screwed up and blew us apart. Still, I loved her and she said she loved me. I figured there was love in her fright.

"You watching the morning news?" I said.

"They've got pictures of you. They're saying you shot a policeman."

"No—well, yeah, but not really."

"Where are you?"

"They've got me at the First District Station. Not in lockup. Yet."

"Joe, what's going on?"

"I'll need to explain later. It's a mess. But I need a favor."

She'd regretted most of the favors she'd done for me in the past but she said, "Anything."

My eleven-year-old nephew had been living with me for the last three months. He would be rolling out of bed about now, wondering why the house was quiet and where I was. "Jason needs breakfast and a ride to school," I said.

She hesitated. "They'll let you go in time to pick him up after school?"

A good point. "Will you call my mom and ask her to take care of him for a couple days?"

She seemed relieved that I hadn't asked her to do it herself. "Sure."

"Thanks," I said. "I owe you."

"You've always owed me and you always will," she said. Then, gently, "Are you all right?"

I lied. "Yeah, I'm fine. Any moment now, they're going to bring me coffee and donuts."

"Joe?" Her tone told me not to screw with her.

"Look, I've just got to go through the process. I'll call as soon as they let me go."

"Do," she said. I imagined her standing over a worktable in the back room of her landscaping business. The bright light and heat of sunlamps would surround her. She would be wearing jeans and short sleeves and her arms would be dusted with potting soil. She would have a dozen green plastic pots on the worktable and she would be transplanting the first growths of flowers and ferns, which she would transplant again into the gardens of her wealthy customers in the spring. I'd seen her like that dozens of times. I wished I was standing with her. I started to tell her that but she'd hung up.

At the other end of the hall a door swung open and a cop guided a short black man my way. The man wore a blue surgical gown but he looked like the closest he'd ever gotten to being a surgeon was when he broke into a doctor's medicine pantry for a fresh supply of OxyContin. He stumbled twice, and, when the cop handcuffed him to a chair down the line from mine and disappeared through the glass door, he kept his eyes on the floor.

I dialed Lucinda Juarez. We'd worked together for the past month, and we'd spent a night together once before that—the worst of the screw-ups that had kept Corrine and me apart. Lucinda was another ex-cop, smarter and quicker than anyone I knew on the force and way smarter and quicker than me. If

Larry Weiss screwed up and left me sitting in jail, I figured I could count on her to do what it took to spring me. I needed her to get started now.

As Lucinda's phone rang the glass door swung open and the woman cop and three uniformed cops came out. She extended her hand for my phone. I gave it to her.

"Time to check into the First District Hotel," she said.

THREE

FOR THREE DAYS I sat in an isolation cell behind the 1st District Station, which had the biggest stationhouse lockup in the city. If a political convention came to town and a demonstration got out of hand, the cops put the protesters there. The rest of the time, the jail housed hookers, pimps, dealers, and addicts. Far as I could tell, the cell block I was in held no one but me.

A little time to myself. Time to think. Time to reflect on my life and the choices I'd made. Not a bad thing, I told myself. Everyone should do it.

That worked for about an hour.

For three days I had no newspaper. No TV. No phone calls. Larry Weiss never managed to get inside to see me. Maybe he was right—maybe I needed a better lawyer. Corrine didn't get in either. Lucinda must've figured out where I was but she never showed. Guards delivered three meals a day, enough to survive on. They shrugged when I asked to see my lawyer. They laughed when I demanded to talk to the district commander. I didn't bother to ask for Corrine or Lucinda. The stainless steel toilet and sink were clean when I arrived but started to stink on the second day. The world outside the stationhouse could've burned and I wouldn't have known.

In the evenings before Jen Horlarche had hired me to watch the Southshore construction site, I'd been reading about a fishing village just over the Florida border from Georgia. Boats went out at night from the mouth of the St. Johns River and came back at dawn, their nets dripping salt back into the ocean, their holds full of shrimp or redfish or both. Winter, spring, summer, and fall, the waves danced in the sunlight where the river met the Atlantic. At the river mouth the undertow got crazy and every year riptides swept two or three people out to sea, waving good-bye to their family and friends on the beach. But the village looked like a place I wanted to be.

If I sold my house, I could afford to rent a moving truck and buy a place big enough for me and Jason—and Corrine, if she would come. I might have enough left over to buy a little boat and some nets. I'd finally decided the fishing village was more than a dream. Then Jen Horlarche had called and invited me to spend my nights in a wasteland where men stole copper. Instead of breathing deep in the warm salt spray, I'd sat in my car and watched dirty plastic sheets blowing across the dirt in the November wind and thieves and cops, who looked identical, shooting each other and my own hand coming away from my holster with my Glock in it. And pulling the trigger.

Every time I'd seen someone die I'd felt the world go a little quieter like I'd lost part of my hearing, and sooner or later the singing, laughing, and screaming would fade into a hushing wind of white noise. That had happened when my dad died. It had happened when Kevin, a boy I was supposed to be protecting, ended up twisted and broken on his mother's kitchen floor. It had happened. Shooting the cop felt worse. I'd ripped a little hole in the universe and I wondered what sound would fly out through it.

For three days I stared at the three cinder-block walls, the bars that formed the fourth wall, and the concrete floor. I stared at myself too but I preferred the walls, floor, and metal bars.

On the afternoon of the fourth day a guard unlocked the cell door and pointed his thumb over his shoulder. "Come on," he said. "Detective Chroler wants to see you." We went through the next cell block where the prisoners jeered and cheered me like they knew something about me that I didn't know. Then we went through two security doors and were back among the living. Cops in uniforms or plainclothes walked the corridor, laughed with each other, or stood outside office doors talking on cell phones. It made me dizzy.

We went around a corner, into a stairwell, and up some stairs. Detective Jane Chroler had an office next to the stairwell. She sat at her desk looking unhappy, though I guessed she had been spending her days and nights in nicer places than I had. A stack of newspapers rested on the corner of her desk with a copy of the morning *Sun-Times* on top. The headline to the lead story read, NO PROGRESS IN SOUTHSHORE KILLINGS. A headline to a sidebar story next to it read, ROGUE INVESTIGATOR JAILED. The article included a small color photograph of me. It was the photograph from my detective's license. In the paper it looked like a mug shot.

I knew Chroler had positioned the newspaper for my benefit. "Sit," she said.

I took the chair across the desk from her, and the guard left us. A steam heater hissed softly, but the tile floor and the walls were bare and the room felt cold.

I said, "Ballistics confirmed what I told you?"

"More or less," she said.

"More or less?"

"You fired your gun once, like you said. The bullet was in Officer Russo, like you said."

"He's the one who was helping the thieves?"

"According to what you've said."

"And who says anything different?"

"No one."

"So where's the 'more or less'?"

"Officer Russo's gun was unloaded."

"Huh?"

She nodded. "You say he aimed it at the other officers, but there were no bullets in it. So why would he do that?"

That made no sense. "He was on duty and his gun was unloaded?"

She shrugged. "A lot else remains unknown. We haven't caught the others. When we do, they might tell us something about you." She kept her eyes on me like she was expecting me to sweat.

The thieves couldn't say anything about me. I sweated anyway. "I don't think they'll tell you anything very interesting."

She cracked a small, mean smile. "I spent a little time over the last three days looking at records and getting to know you. And I've got to say, I don't like you. When you were in the department you had a habit of breaking the rules and the habit got worse after you were fired. You're a drunk. You use drugs. You—"

"I quit all that a long time ago."

"Number one rule of AA: Once a drunk, always a drunk. You might not be drinking but you're still a drunk, just waiting for life to get bad enough again to start you up again. Same thing for an addict, from what I've seen. Never a cure, just occasional vacations."

I gave her a hard stare. It didn't make her sweat.

She frowned. "This isn't the first time you've been present when a cop has gotten shot, is it?"

"You know it isn't."

"You know where Detective Gubman is now?"

Two months earlier, my friend Bill Gubman had asked me to go with him to stake out and ID a robbery suspect I'd seen. I couldn't ID the guy, but he'd shot Bill in the stomach. If I'd moved faster, I could've shot the suspect first. It was getting to be an old story.

Bill had spent three weeks in the hospital and another three in rehab. The doctors had taken out half of his upper colon and a couple other spare parts, but he'd lived. Far as I knew, he was at home recovering with his wife Eileen.

I said so to Chroler.

She shook her head. "First day back. He's sitting at a desk downstairs."

That made me happy, kind of. "Welcome him back for me."

She shook her head some more. "He hates that desk. But that's where he'll be until he retires."

I said, "Are you letting me go?"

"Got no reason to keep you."

"You had no reason to keep me for three days."

She shrugged. "We forgot about you."

"I wish."

"You need a better lawyer." She reached under her desk, came up with a plastic bag, slid the bag across the desk to me.

I laid the contents on the desktop. My cell phone, the battery dead. My keys. My holster—without my Glock.

"My gun?" I asked.

"Impounded."

My wallet. I flipped it open. Four twenties, a five, and two ones inside—probably what I was carrying when the police took it from me. Also my Visa card and driver's license.

Something was missing.

"My detective's license?"

"Under review," Chroler said, like it was no big deal.

"What's that mean?" There was no review process that the police were part of, not that I knew of. "The Department of Professional Regulation handles complaints, you don't. Only the DPR can revoke a license."

"The DPR gave this one to us."

"Bullshit. They don't do that."

Chroler shrugged. "Your license is under review."

Fighting with her would get me nowhere. I would ask Larry to do what he could. Or I would get a better lawyer.

I stood up.

"Take the newspapers too," Chroler said. "You might learn something."

"About?"

"Yourself."

I picked up the newspapers, turned to go, stopped at the doorway. "You could have had me released downstairs. Why did you call me up here?"

"I wanted to give you the newspapers personally. Also I wanted to be the first to tell you that one of the wounded officers died. So that's three dead now and two still in the hospital. Congratulations."

FOUR

THEY'D PARKED MY SKYLARK at the curb outside the station. Couldn't do better with a parking attendant. They hadn't washed it, though.

I sat in my car and fingered through the newspapers while the November sky grayed against the afternoon.

The first copy of the *Sun-Times* ran a front-page headline that said SOUTHSIDE MASSACRE and showed pictures of the five men killed and wounded. David Russo, Tom Stanley, and Marvin du Pont, dead. Christopher Pelman and Emelio Fernandez, wounded. The article said they were experienced, dedicated cops. It mentioned the thefts at the construction site but didn't say that officers Russo and Stanley were in with the thieves. According to a police spokesman quoted by the paper, all five were heroes who died or had been wounded protecting the city. The spokesman also said the thieves had gotten away in two dark-colored vans. A third van, left behind, was stolen. As far as the newspaper reporter seemed to know, I didn't exist.

The *Tribune* had the same information, though it included a diagram showing where the cops fell and biographical sketches of the dead and wounded. David Russo, the cop I'd shot when he pointed his gun at the others, was married but had no kids. I breathed easier at the no-kids part. But his sister said he'd grown up wanting to be a cop like his dad, a story I knew too well.

By the third morning, frustration was starting to show. The *Sun-Times* ran a sidebar titled BLOODBATHS IN BLUE about the psychological effects of shootings on the men and women in blue. They'd also gotten my name and described me as a private investigator who'd phoned the police with news of the Southshore robbery. They mentioned that I had a checkered past but other than that they left me alone.

The *Tribune* was ahead of them. They'd gotten their hands on the 911 tape of me reporting the Southshore theft and broke the news that officers Russo and Stanley were involved in it. They said I was an ex-cop with a drinking problem. They'd dug through their files and come up with a photo of the newsstand I'd wiped out with my cruiser the night before the department fired me. Last time I'd seen the photo it was deep in the Local News section of the paper. Now it was page one.

This morning's *Sun-Times* went hard into the story about departmental corruption, questioning if only Russo and Stanley were involved in the thefts. An op-ed article noted that no one had been arrested, wondered about a conspiracy of silence in the department, and called for an investigation. In the "Rogue Investigator" story, Detective Jane Chroler called me a *person of interest*. The article also connected me to Bill Gubman's shooting two months earlier.

The *Tribune* article gave most of the same information and provided a time line of the shootings and investigation. It called me a *person of interest* again, said I was in jail, un-charged, quoted Larry Weiss calling me innocent, reminded readers of my drinking habit, and quoted an unnamed former detective calling me "dirty."

I dropped the stack of papers onto the passenger-side floor. Dirty.

I pulled my car into traffic. Across the street, a woman with a German shepherd was going into a redbrick building that had a sign advertising dog boarding, grooming, and training. The building had steel doors and glass-block windows that started about eight feet up from the pavement. Another prison. A white Honda SUV pulled from the curb in front of the build-ing, made a U-turn, and fell in behind me.

At the corner, I turned west onto 18th Street and cruised in the shadow of the El tracks. I checked the rearview mirror. The SUV followed me. We crossed the brown water of the old Sani-tary and Ship Canal—the rusting steel skeleton of a railway bridge in the near distance, the downtown skyscrapers beyond it. We crossed the tracks of an empty railroad yard. We passed vacant lots with broken-down trucks and piles of scrap.

The stoplight at Canal Street turned red. Afternoon rush hour was starting even in a lousy part of the city like this, and the SUV pulled close behind me. My rearview mirror showed two men. They looked thirty or thirty-five, both with short, re-ceding dark hair that they'd messed up so it needed a comb. One of them wore black, the other a camouflage jacket. Like anyone still wore camouflage. That probably made them plain-clothes cops. They stared out the windshield with faraway eyes as if I wasn't there, which meant they probably were watching me close.

I waited until the line of cross traffic approached, then

punched the accelerator. The truck at the front of the line blew its horn but I slipped in front of it. The SUV lurched and tried to follow. It had nowhere to go.

My car shot up Canal, past an old warehouse converted into a self-storage business, then past factories and more vacant lots. I searched the rearview mirror. Far as I could tell, the SUV was a half mile away.

There were no stoplights on this stretch of Canal. I blew forward to Roosevelt Road, swung around the corner, and headed east. More railroad tracks. Back across the Sanitary and Ship Canal. More vacant lots. Across Clark Street, and suddenly million-dollar condos, tennis courts, and trees surrounded me. I sighed, let the tension go.

Then I glanced at the mirror.

The white SUV had fallen in two cars back.

Traffic had thickened but the SUV wedged into the right lane and pulled within a car length. I wondered what the rush was. The men had caught up with me, so they must've figured out where I was heading to begin with. The SUV slid back into my lane, with a VW between us.

The stoplight at State Street turned red and I hit the brakes. I considered getting out, tapping on the driver's window, telling the men to get lost, but the SUV pulled into the left-turn lane, rolled next to me, stopped.

The passenger-side window rolled down. The man in the black jacket gave me a tight-lipped smile.

I rolled down my window, said, "What the hell—"

He lifted a black pistol, pointed it at my head.

I didn't need to think. My body moved on its own. My hand reached for my holster.

No gun in it.

I looked for a way out to the left, right, front, and back. Cars boxed me in.

The pistol fired—a huge sound. My vision narrowed.

I waited for the pain, thought I felt it coming. Where? I wiped my hands over my face, stared at them. No blood.

The SUV pulled away, bounced over a concrete median, completed a U-turn, and disappeared behind me.

The other cars didn't move, though the light had turned green. A big man climbed out of a red Camry and ran toward me, shouting. I watched his hands for a weapon, saw none. Was he with the men in the SUV, coming to finish me off? I looked around frantically. What could I hit him with? My cell phone? A shoe? A newspaper?

He was outside my window, shouting. What was he saying? I forced myself to listen.

"Are—you—all—right?"

I ran my hands down my ribs, over my belly. No pain. I put my hands on my neck, looked at my arms and legs. No blood.

"Are you all right?" the man was asking.

I stared at him, said nothing.

He leaned toward me, his hands on my door, his fingers curling through the open window. "Are you—?"

I lifted his fingers away from my car with my fingers. I rolled up the window.

He was a good man, a saint.

I had nothing to say to him, no use for him at all.

The cars in front moved. The man stepped away from my Skylark, bewildered. I let my car roll forward, accelerated through the intersection.

The next corner was Wabash. I turned, drove up the street, and turned again into a parking lot.

I cut the engine and breathed deep. The air felt thin. I tried to think—until a single simple idea grew bright. *It was time to hide.*

If the guys in the SUV were plainclothes, and I was pretty sure they were, then the cops were gunning for me. I could argue my innocence any way I wanted but I'd killed a man in uniform, thief or not—and the man, if not quite unarmed, had an unloaded weapon and couldn't have shot it even if he'd wanted to. That would be enough to drive some guys in the department crazy.

It was time to hide.

How had the shooter in the SUV missed me? He was five feet away, four maybe. If he'd had long arms, he could've punched me without getting out of his car. How could he have missed?

Where could I hide?

I knew about a little fishing village just over the Florida border.

I also knew a store two doors from the entrance to the building where I had my office. The store advertised BEER, WINE, LIQUOR. LOWEST PRICES. It had no other name. A Polish guy named Charlie Brzowski used to run it. When I still was drinking, he knew my face better than my mom did. He was bald and heavy and picked up the bottle some himself.

I got out of my car. The bullet shot by the man in the SUV had poked a hole through the panel behind the driver-side door. Like a thumb through a pie.

The shooter had meant to miss me. He'd meant only to scare.

I looked inside the car. The bullet had stopped short of the interior paneling. It was under the skin and might rattle, metal against metal, when I drove, but it would hurt me only as much as I let it.

I locked the car.

Charlie Brzowski was gone from the liquor store. A thin Indian man stood behind the counter. He wore his green shirt buttoned to the neck and had a full head of black hair. Still the store smelled and felt the same, and the bourbon was where it always had been. I grabbed a bottle of Jim Beam Black—good but not too good.

My office was on the eighth floor of an eight-story building. A secretarial school that taught inner-city kids occupied the rest of the floor. I rode the elevator up alone. Roselle Turner, who owned and ran the school, was in her office talking on the phone as I walked by, but the students had left for the day.

A steel plate on my office door said JOE KOZMARSKI. PRVATE INVESTIGATION AND DETECTIVE SERVICES. I resisted tearing it off.

A pile of letters, bills, and take-out menus sat on the floor. Other than that, the office looked like it always did: the desk, the computer, the answering machine blinking red to tell me I had calls, the metal file cabinets, the couch where I'd some-times slept until my nephew Jason had come to live with me. I set the Jim Beam on the desk and went to the window. On a clear day, Lake Michigan showed through a gap between an insurance building and the building to the north of it. It showed now but the gray of the lake blended with the gray of the sky so it didn't much matter.

I picked up the mail and sat at my desk.

The menus and credit card offers went into the trash. The bills went into a separate pile, unopened. A letter on legal sta-tionery explained that a client who'd hired me to tell her where her husband was spending his evenings wouldn't be paying my bill because she was unsatisfied with my services. I'd followed her husband but the news that he was spending his after-work hours playing chess with an old high school friend didn't deserve payment, as far as my client was concerned. She'd been sure he was gambling or screwing another woman and wanted me to confirm her suspicions as badly as she worried about the truth of them.

An envelope stamped with the Southshore Corporation logo contained a letter from Jen Horlarche telling me my security services would no longer be required. It was a Dear John letter, polite enough as those things go. At the bottom, she noted that she'd sent a copy to the Southshore legal counsel.

The last envelope had no return address. Inside were a little Baggie and a note. The note said, *Sorry about the bad luck. Let me know what you need.—Tommy.* The signature made me shudder. Tommy had supplied my needs when I'd had habits that needed supplying. I hadn't seen him or heard from him since I'd broken the habits. Now that the news showed me washing down a storm drain, he was reaching a hand to pull me out. Drowning would be better.

I tapped the Baggie to settle its contents. Inside was enough cocaine to make three or four lines. Enough to get me started. When I needed more, I could call Tommy.

I balled up the Baggie and threw it in the garbage.

I looked at my desk, saw the bottle of Jim Beam.

What was I doing?

I dropped the bottle into the can on top of the Baggie.

I closed my eyes, breathed deep.

I waited for the tension to pass, breathed deep again, waited some more, breathed again.

What was I doing?

I pulled the bottle out of the garbage, set it on my desk, reached in again for the Baggie, and put it into my top desk drawer.

I watched the bottle as though it would talk to me.

Then I unscrewed the cap and took a drink, felt the burn and the release and the bright solution to every problem.

It was time to hide.

FIVE

THE PHONE WAS RINGING.

Someone should answer it.

Not me.

The phone rang some more.

I drank.

The machine picked up, explained I was unavailable. An understatement.

My ex-wife Corrine spoke, her voice worried. "I talked with Larry Weiss. He says the police told him they released you. I left a message for you at home, and your cell phone seems to be off. Where are you?"

I'm not here, I thought.

"I'm concerned about you," she added and hung up.

Yeah, me too.

I left what remained of the whiskey on my desk, went out of my office, locked the door. Roselle Turner was still in her office, talking on the phone.

The elevator took me down to the street. The first dark of the evening had fallen. Streetlights and shop lights washed the pavement yellow. A couple of taxis, some passenger cars, and a city bus passed me on Wabash. I shouldn't drive. The vendors in the newsstands that I hadn't flattened agreed I shouldn't. I walked toward my car.

A police cruiser came around the corner, slowed.

Panic flooded my belly. I fought it off, kept walking. I knew better than to think that every cop in the city had it out for me.

The cruiser pulled to the curb and two cops got out. "Mr. Kozmarski?" one of the cops said.

I kept walking, pretended I was someone else.

"Mr. Kozmarski?" The voice was closer.

If I ran, I would have no chance. I was drunk, tired. Maybe if I sat on the sidewalk, they would leave me alone.

"Mr.—"

I turned. "What?"

The cop almost ran into me. "We need you to come with us."

I looked him in the eyes. He was a couple of inches shorter than my six feet but thick in the shoulders and arms, like he spent his off-hours at the gym. His partner stood behind him, about the same height but thinner, his hand on his hip near his service pistol.

"No," I said.

My refusal didn't seem to bother them. They seemed to think it was funny.

The lead cop held his hands together over his chest. He could pray if he wanted to. Or he could throw a forearm into my jaw.

He said, "Bill Gubman wants to talk to you."

Lieutenant Detective Bill Gubman—my closest friend in the department and maybe outside it too. We'd gone through the academy together, stood side by side at graduation, and become rookies in the same district. We fell away from each other for awhile when the department fired me. But then he called one night, crazy worried about his wife Eileen, and asked me to connect her with the substance-abuse counselor who'd helped me with my habits. Then we were close again. But two months ago he'd taken a bullet I should've stopped, and now I had a tank full of Jim Beam, and three or four lines of coke waiting for me in my desk drawer.

"I've got nothing to say to him," I said.

"I didn't ask if you did. I said he wants to talk to you."

I shook my head, turned away.

They came at me fast, grabbed my arms, and threw me against a building. I tasted brick. I could've fought but saw no use in it. They cuffed my hands behind my back and shoved me toward their cruiser, the headlights of passing cars in my eyes. Fifteen minutes later, we pulled into a spot at the 1st District Station. The place was starting to feel like home.

Bill Gubman sat at a desk on the first floor. The plaque outside his door called him Liaison to the Board of Ethics. The Board of Ethics was an independent unit in the city government, set up after a *Sun-Times* series of articles exposed three cases of corruption in the department's own internal affairs division and a citizen action group collected over a hundred thousand signatures calling for external oversight. Now, when a cop used too much force against a citizen, or stole copper wire from a construction site, or got wasted and plowed his cruiser into a newsstand, the board made sure the department cleaned the dirt instead of just sweeping it out of sight. The department had a number of liaisons who kept relations with the board happy and sometimes alerted department higher-ups in time to sweep dirt out of the way before the board could point it out. The liaison job was a cushy chair reserved for guys too burned out to return to the street but who were a few months or a couple years short of pension, or guys who'd taken a bullet in the line of duty but were too restless to stay at home watching *Oprah* on administrative leave.

The job was a long way from the homicide squad where Bill had worked for the past twelve years and I figured the cushy chair would be chafing him.

The cop who'd cuffed me unlocked my hands outside the door and knocked.

Bill waved me in and signaled to the cop to close the door behind me. His cold face said nothing about the meals I'd eaten at his house or the ones he and his wife had eaten at mine. He sat uncomfortably at his desk. His body had the lopsided shape of a man who'd gotten wounded in the gut and the surgical patchwork was tugging on one side, or else something was missing in the middle and he couldn't help sagging into it.

"Have a seat," he said.

I shook my head. "I'll stand."

His lips twitched like an unseen pain stabbed him, but he stared hard at me.

I shrugged and sat in the chair across the desk from him.

He said, "In the eighteen years that Professional Regulations has been keeping track, you know what percentage of licensed private detectives have been disciplined?"

I shrugged again.

"Just over seven percent. Mostly it's for something small—

improper completion of an affidavit or, at worst, impersonation of a peace officer. The PIs do their probation and return to active status or they move on to something else." He kept the hard eyes on me. "You're the first private detective to shoot a police officer, clean or dirty. No one else like you on the record books. What do you think will happen to you?"

I knew he was doing his job, figured he might even have asked someone to assign me to him so the bad news could come from a friend. Still, I didn't like bad news.

I gestured toward his gut. "How are you feeling, Bill?"

"Fuck how I'm feeling. You don't shoot a cop, even a bad cop, and go back to work. Not in this city."

"I understand," I said.

He sighed. "What were you thinking?"

"I wasn't thinking. I was just dealing with the situation as well as I could."

He cracked a grim smile. "You know, after I took a bullet and now this, a lot of guys around here think you've got a grudge against cops and you're gunning for us. Evidence looks pretty strong to a lot of them. These guys think you need to be stopped."

I thought about the white Honda SUV. "Yeah, I've maybe met a couple of them."

He let that pass. "So the smart thing to do would be to leave town. Go fishing for a month or two. Or longer, much longer. You can run away now but I don't know about later. I say this as a friend."

I'd never told him about the Florida fishing village but he seemed to know. Maybe we all had a place like that. "And what do you say as a cop?"

He sat back, folded his hands gently over his lopsided belly.

He stared at me awhile like he was putting words to his thoughts. "There's another option," he said. "Right now, you look dirty. Hell, with all the shit that flew at Southshore Village, you *are* dirty. You could make that dirt work for you—and for us."

"Tell me."

Again the long stare. "You remember a guy named Earl Johnson?"

"Sure. He was in our academy class—a bit of a screwup. Barely made it through. He did all right afterward, though. Vice detective, last I heard."

"Still on vice, though he spent a few years on the gang unit before that." Bill looked at me square. "He's behind the Southshore thefts."

I shook my head. "He wasn't there."

"Not there, but he was behind it. He leads a group of eight other cops—ten until our guys dropped one of them and you dropped the other. They're into anything that makes money. Mostly industrial theft and prostitution. Industrial theft because one of them has a brother-in-law who owns a reprocessing company. Prostitution because of Johnson's vice connections. We've been aware of them for the last eight months, and we've gotten a good sense of who's involved and what they're doing. Right now, they're getting greedier and trying to expand."

He pushed a stack of photos across the desk. They included nine men. Earl Johnson was one of them. I recognized another two as the guys who'd shot at me from the white Honda SUV. The four guys who'd driven into the Southshore construction site and loaded copper wire into their vans until I called 911 were there too. In the pictures they wore police uniforms.

I pulled out the four photos and put them on the desk. "These guys were there."

Bill nodded. "We know."

"So arrest them and you're done."

"Not that easy. If the size of this group goes public, the department is screwed. We'll be busy for the next ten years explaining that we're not Juarez, Mexico, with cops playing both sides of the law. The mayor doesn't want that. The chief doesn't want that. Fuck knows, I don't want it."

"This is what you do for the Ethics Board?" I said.

"If the Ethics Board found out, they wouldn't want it either. Too big. Too messy. Everybody wants these guys to disappear."

"That's where I come in?"

Bill nodded, picked up the stack of photos, and pulled out a picture of a dark-skinned, balding man. "This guy here, his name's Bob Monroe. Also on vice. Used to be on the gang unit, which is where he met Johnson. Last summer he went toe-to-toe with Johnson for control of the group. Lost out to him and he's unhappy—doesn't like being number two and he's looking for an excuse to make a move. Most of the other guys don't trust him, though. He comes across at first like a nice guy but he's crazy. When he was on the gang unit he had a run-in with a kid named Victor Lopez. Victor started talking to the Ethics Board, but then he disappeared—with some unwanted help from Monroe. We couldn't find even a bone fragment. The other guys know Monroe's a hothead but he thinks they'll line up behind him if he takes Johnson down."

"What do you see me doing?"

He handed me the photo. "You give Monroe news about

times, dates, and places that Johnson has been running operations outside the group and pocketing the money. You give him the specific amounts he's ripped off. You tell Monroe you've come across the information in your private investigations into the group. I give you the list and the evidence. Johnson will have no alibi. We know where he was at the times and we've set up dummy bank accounts in his name. The money will be there when Monroe checks for it. Monroe will make a move on Johnson. Johnson will fight it. My guess is Johnson will end up dead on the street and the others will run and hide their heads instead of getting behind Monroe. If not, we'll play man against man till they're so busy dancing they won't have time for stealing or pimping."

"Seems to me a lot riskier than arresting them."

"If you listen to the superintendent and mayor, nothing's riskier than arresting them. For once, I agree with them. Way too much bad publicity. This is the kind of thing that could define the department and the city for years." He stared at me again. "This is straightforward undercover work but a cop can't do it. The guys in the group would be too suspicious, especially right now. But you—they'll know you're independent, and after the Southshore shootings they'll think you're gutsy enough to make this kind of move." He said it with a smile but I knew better.

"I'm already tied to the deaths of two of them," I said. "Why would they want to talk to me?"

"Trust me, they want to talk. You're the only one who saw them at Southshore. They need to find out what you know. My guess is they'll pick you up off the street for a conversation and you can make your case for partnering with them. If not, you get in touch with them yourself, tell them you've dug them up as part of your investigation and you're interested in making a deal. Your job as a detective is gone, you need an income, you're impressed by the work they do, etcetera."

"They'll kill me."

"Probably not. They could use a guy like you."

"I walk in, disasters happen."

He nodded. "It's a talent."

"What does Detective Chroler think about this?" I asked.

"She's signed on," he said. "You'll never hear from her again." He gave me a long stare. "What do you think?"

"What's in it for me?"

"Your life back. Chroler takes her thumb off the top of your head. The department leaves you alone. You get to live on your own terms again."

If I pulled off the job, I would have a chance at redeeming myself. The Department of Professional Regulation might even let me keep my detective's license. "I think I'll go fishing," I said.

He looked at me long again, then smiled. "That's what I would do if I were you."

I smiled too. "No, you wouldn't. You could be lounging on a beach right now, expenses paid by the city. You could milk your injury for six months or a year before coming back, no questions asked. But you're working twelve-hour days if I know you, worrying Eileen because you won't take it easy."

We smiled at each other for awhile, eyes on each other's eyes, neither of us blinking.

Then I said, "Did you tell a *Tribune* reporter I'm dirty?"

He blinked. "Never."

I nodded, waited for him to blink again. He didn't. I said, "You want to bring Eileen to my house for dinner?"

He seemed to pull into himself. He said, "When this is over, okay?"

SIX

I TOLD BILL I would find my own way home.

A five-minute walk from the front of the station would take me to the Velvet Lounge on Cermak Road, shouldered between a Vietnamese manicure business and Baba's Restaurant, the only place in the city advertising FAMOUS STEAK & LEMONADE. You would never guess from the clean redbrick building housing the Velvet Lounge that inside you could hear the raunchiest jazz in Chicago. The music wouldn't start for another two hours. But the Velvet Lounge also poured a tall shot. That was enough for me.

When I left the station a white Honda SUV with tinted windows idled at the curb. A shiver ran down my back. I fought it off. Chicago had to have thousands of white Honda SUVs. I was crazy to think this was the same one that had tailed me when I got out of jail.

I crossed the street, turned south, walked toward Cermak. Two men got out of the SUV and followed me on the other side.

One wore a camouflage jacket, the other black. The guy in black had short, receding dark hair. The guy in camouflage wore a gray wool skullcap, though I figured he had hair that matched the other guy's.

I sped up.

They sped up.

I could run but I figured they could run faster.

The evening wind came from the south. If you looked for its tail, maybe you would find it in a quiet Florida fishing village. But it stung cold. The passing headlights were cold. On November evenings like this in Chicago everything was cold.

I kept to the east side of the street, passing businesses that looked like they'd been dying since the 1970s—Blue Star Auto Store, Super Deal Food & Liquor, Giant Slice Pizza. The two men stayed across the street, where developers had knocked down old buildings and built gated condos and landscaped high-rises. The one in the black coat talked on a cell phone.

At the corner of Cermak, I went left and they trotted across the street and followed me under the El tracks. At Wabash, a plastic sign advertising MUFFLERS 4 LESS banged in the wind. I crossed, passed a place that sold POLLO AL CARBON through an outside walk-up window, and slipped into the Velvet Lounge.

If the guys from the SUV wanted to join me for a drink, I would buy them a round. If they wanted to shoot me, there wasn't a lot I could do to stop them.

At a quarter to seven on a cold November evening, the Velvet Lounge was almost empty. A recording of Coleman Hawkins played on the stereo. The room smelled like spilled liquor. The paneling on the walls was blond pressboard and the posters of jazz greats were framed in plastic, but the bar top was heavy oak covered with polished glass. Behind it, liquor bottles stood in an art deco display. The place put its money where it mattered.

As I sat on a stool, the door swung open and the men from the SUV came in. They sat at a table facing me. A pistol showed on the hip of the guy in black, and, if you bothered to look, the camouflage jacket bulged over a shoulder holster.

The bartender, a brown-skinned man in jeans and a black guayabera shirt, brought me a shot of Early Times and a glass of water. A waitress with blond, stringy hair took care of the men at the table. She had a low-cut blouse and leaned over their table like she expected them to tuck ten-dollar bills inside, but they kept their eyes on me.

When we had our drinks, I considered leaving mine on the bar, going to the men's room, slipping through a window, and catching a taxi for the airport. I had enough cash for cab fare and a credit card would take me the rest of the way.

I stood with my whiskey and brought it to the table where the men were sitting. I sat down across from them. They didn't seem surprised by my company.

I drank the shot, let its burn warm my throat and stomach, felt the heat rise to my head. "Okay," I said. "What now?"

The man in black said, "We're worried about you, Joe."

"My ex-wife's worried about me too. Maybe we could start a club. Like a fan club but with hand wringing."

He shook his head. "Don't be a smart-ass. It doesn't work for you."

"I'm sitting at a table with two guys who put a bullet in the rear panel of my car, and I have the feeling these guys are cops who undoubtedly can explain why the bullet is in my car in a way that doesn't involve them personally. Basically I'm screwed if you want me to be. So being a smart-ass is all I've got."

"The key is that we shot the bullet into the rear panel instead of your head. So you could try a little humility."

The bartender watched our table like he knew something was wrong, but he didn't reach for the telephone. Not yet.

"What do you want from me?" I said. "You want to scare me? You've done it and can go home. You want something else, you'd better talk fast because I'm planning to drink until I can't hear you anymore."

I signaled to the bartender and tapped my shot glass.

The guy in camouflage said, "You made a big mess at Southshore. It's the kind of mess that you can't clean up. So, you just need to build on top of it as if it isn't there. You understand?"

"Not in the least," I said.

He said, "If you want, we can forget about what happened at Southshore. We can start from here."

Nothing I would like better. "Why would you want to do that?"

"Three good cops are dead, two wounded. Nothing you can do to change that now. Nothing we can do either. So why bother trying? We'll move on."

"Three *good* cops?" I repeated.

"That's right."

The bartender brought my drink. He looked me in the eyes—close, like he was waiting for me to signal him to call for help. Instead, I tipped him a couple bucks.

When he went back behind the bar, I asked, "Have you guys got names?"

"Peter Finley," said the guy in camouflage.

"Farid el Raj," said the other. "Call me Raj."

A young couple came through the door into the bar laughing. They walked toward the table next to ours, looked us over, then sat. Peter Finley shook his head like he couldn't believe their stupidity.

I downed my shot and signaled to the bartender for another.

"So, what now?" I said.

"Now we help each other. You need to talk to one of our friends."

"Yeah? Who's that?"

I figured they would say Earl Johnson, the head of their crew, but they named number two, the guy who Bill Gubman said wanted to challenge Johnson. "Bob Monroe. You know who he is?"

"I've heard of him," I said.

The waitress brought my drink. The bartender had given up on me.

I reached for it but Finley put his hand on top of it. "Let's go," he said.

He and Raj stood.

I didn't want to get into a car with these guys. Maybe they wanted information about how much I'd told Detective Chroler and Bill Gubman. Maybe they would do whatever they needed to do to get it and then they would kill me. Why not? Two of their own were already dead, a good cop was dead with them, and two more were wounded. What was one disgraced private detective? No one forgave as easily as they said.

I stood. "Give me a minute," I said. "I need to use the bathroom."

SEVEN

A SIGN ON THE back exit said an alarm would ring if I opened the door. I turned the handle. No alarm. The alley outside was dark and dirty, but two taxis were passing as I stepped out to the sidewalk. I flagged the second.

My cell phone rang while it was speeding up the Dan Ryan toward the Kennedy Expressway. Eighteen miles from O'Hare Airport. Twenty minutes at this time of night.

The display said the caller was unknown, which meant the phone probably was disposable—and untraceable. I knew I shouldn't answer. The voice on the other end wouldn't be calling to wish me bon voyage.

A clean break, that's what I needed. I should turn off my phone and drop it in the trash outside the airport.

But there's no such thing as a clean break. I knew that too.

I answered.

"What the fuck do you think you're doing?" Finley, the guy in camouflage, yelled into the phone.

"Running," I said. The truth seemed as good as a lie.

That stopped him for only a moment. "First, you can't run. We'll find you wherever you go. Second, we know about you. We know about your mother and her little house on Leland. We know about your ex-wife. Pretty lady. We know about your nephew, the one who's been living with you. Looks like a nice kid."

He didn't need to make the threat explicit.

"You still at the Velvet Lounge?" I said.

"Out front."

"I'll be there in ten minutes."

"Make it sooner."

When I told the cabdriver to turn around and take me back, he shrugged and mumbled, "You must be nuts."

I didn't argue.

THE WHITE SUV WAS idling outside of the Velvet Lounge. Raj and Finley stood next to it. Raj patted me down for a weapon, then opened the back passenger door and I climbed in.

Peter Finley climbed into the driver's seat and Raj got in beside him.

We cruised quietly toward downtown. The SUV smelled like new leather upholstery and men's sweat. I looked from man to man. They sat silent and calm like we were out for an evening and the excitement wouldn't start until we reached our destination.

Traffic thickened.

"You guys take a lot of risks," I said.

They didn't seem to think that needed an answer.

I said, "Sooner or later a security camera's going to catch you. Or you'll run into nightshift at a construction site and they'll see you. Your friends in the department won't need to look at mug shots. They'll recognize you. Seems like a dumb way of working."

Finley said, "This from a man who falls asleep on a job and then wakes up and shoots a cop."

I shut up.

The wheels sounded like rushing water on the pavement. The city lights glared through the windows. Finley pulled out a cell phone, punched some numbers, mumbled into the phone, and hung up.

At the corner of Randolph and Michigan, we pulled onto a driveway that dropped into a parking garage below a building called The Winchester. A banner stretching up the side of the building advertised CONDOMINIUMS, APARTMENTS, OFFICES. LAKE VIEWS. We went down two levels and parked by a service elevator.

"Out," said Raj.

We stood in the concrete cavern, a man on each side of me. They knew I was willing to run and weren't taking chances.

The elevator came. Furniture pads lined the walls. We got in. Safe as a padded cell. Someone could get beaten to death in an elevator like this, and who would hear? Raj pushed the button for the twelfth floor.

"You hungry?" Raj said as we rode up.

It was 8:15 and I hadn't eaten since breakfast in jail. Still, the question—from a man who'd shot a bullet into my car, threatened my ex-wife, mother, and nephew, and abducted me off the street—amazed me. "No," I said.

"Too bad."

Bob Monroe's apartment was more or less what you would expect a cop to live in if he was single, had fifteen or twenty years under his belt, and liked to be close to downtown night-life. It was a one bedroom, with a living room-dining room combination, carpeted wall to wall with the beige tough-grade stuff that lasts from tenant to tenant. On the outside wall, sliding glass doors gave a city view. If you stood on the little balcony on the other side of the doors you probably could see the lake.

The dining room table was set for four. Two roasted chickens stood on a platter. A large bowl held baked potatoes, wrapped in foil. Another large bowl held salad. A big glass bucket had what looked like a twelve-pack of Heineken on ice.

Bob Monroe came in from the kitchen with a big smile.

"Welcome!" His voice was as big as he was. He was in his early fifties, black, with an almost bald head, the remaining hair shaved short.

He reached out a big hand to shake.

I ignored it, said, "You're having a dinner party?"

He laughed, though I saw nothing funny. "Just dinner. Thought you might like to join us."

"Not really, no."

Another laugh. "Have a seat at the end."

We sat, me at the end.

Monroe cut up and served the chickens, passed the potatoes and salad. Then, using the carving knife, he cut a large bite of the chicken on his plate and forked it into his mouth. He chewed and asked offhandedly, "So why are you talking with Bill Gubman?"

I looked at my plate. The chicken was steaming, the potato too. Solid food would do me good. I reached for the ice bucket, opened a beer, and drank.

"He's an old friend," I said. "From long ago."

He nodded like he knew it. "It might be time to make new friends."

I cut a bite of chicken, put it in my mouth. It was hot, the marinated skin crispy. I felt almost grateful. "That's what he said."

Monroe smiled. "Yeah?"

"Yeah. He doesn't like dirt. I'm dirty. His words."

"Some friend," Raj said.

Monroe looked thoughtful. "The first twenty-four hours after the Southshore mess, we expected shit to fly. All you had to do was identify us and there'd be a late-night knock at the door and that would be that. I didn't sleep for expecting it."

Raj and Finley nodded. They hadn't been at the Southshore site but they seemed to have gone sleepless too.

Monroe said, "Then twenty-four hours became forty-eight, and we were wondering when everything was going to come down. Then forty-eight became seventy-two, and we started wondering if you'd talked and if you hadn't why not." He looked me in the eyes. "No reason you shouldn't talk. You're in deep, and talking's the only way you're getting out. But we listen around the department and we read the newspaper, and, holy fuck, it looks like you're not talking." He leaned toward me. "So, you know what our question is. Why not?"

Because no one asked me to, I thought. They'd left me alone in the cell. Anyway, as Bill Gubman had told me, at least a few people in the department already knew who had been at the Southshore site. "They threw me in jail and I don't like jail," I said. "I saw no reason to help."

"Even if it meant you stayed up to your chin in shit?"

"Even then."

He sat back. "And what did you say to Gubman today?"

"Before or after he called me dirty?"

"Both."

"Before, I shook his hand and said I was glad to see him. After, I told him to fuck off."

Raj and Peter Finley laughed at that. Bob Monroe just nodded.

Then we ate. I wanted to refuse the food, but I didn't.

The men ragged each other about the women they were dating. They ragged about the evening supervisor on the vice squad. They ragged about the Bears, who'd lost again.

They could have been guys anywhere on a night out, catching up, bullshitting.

Then Monroe leaned back from his plate and said to me, "You know how many gang members there are in Chicago?"

I shook my head no.

"National Youth Gang Survey says almost seventy thousand."

Raj said, "Like a little island nation. Third world."

Monroe nodded. "But you know, even third-world island nations have economies. Think of what you could do if you could mobilize seventy thousand."

I looked at him hard. "What could you do?"

"First of all, there's forty-two gangs in the city, maybe a couple more. But just four of them are really big—the Black Gangster Disciple Nation, the Maniac Latin Disciples, the Latin Kings, and the Vice Lords. Between the four of them, you've got the majority of the gang members—let's say, between thirty-five and forty thousand. So, what would it look like if we ignored the other thirty-eight gangs and gave the big four some structure and rules?"

Again, I said, "What?"

"It would look like business. Like a well-organized business. Right now, the guys on the street know their own crews but they don't know the guys in the other crews and they don't know the guys on top. Same thing from the top down—they don't know the guys on the street. See what I'm getting at?"

"No. Seems to me that the way things are keeps them safe. The bottom guys can't inform on the top."

Monroe shook his head. "They could be safer. They need organization. They need structure. They need protection. That's where we come in."

"At what cost to them?"

Like a salesman, he said, "A very low price—a very good deal for what they get in return. Let's say we can't reach all the gang members in the city. Let's say that even by working with the leaders we can reach only a third of them—twenty-five thousand. Let's say each of those twenty-five thousand brings in just a little bit each day, a buck or two even—say, ten bucks a week. That's two hundred fifty thousand dollars a week. Or let's be conservative. Three out of five of the gangbangers we reach forget to show up with their ten bucks. We're down to a hundred thousand a week."

Peter Finley said, "You can do a hell of a lot on a hundred thousand a week."

Monroe nodded. "A hell of a lot."

I said, "And what do they get in return?"

Monroe said, "They get left alone a lot of the time. We protect anyone whose name is on the list, and we arrest anyone whose isn't. So we take out the competition. Cheap price for that."

I took my last bite of chicken and pushed my chair back like Monroe's. "They'll never pay."

"Yes they will, because the price keeps getting higher if they don't."

I shook my head. "My guess is, in less than a week, one of the gang members would inform on you."

Monroe smiled. "It works already on a small scale. The key is to deal only with the leaders. They've got as much to lose as anyone and they're a hell of a lot smarter than you'd think."

I eyed the remaining piece of chicken, a wing. "What's this got to do with me?"

Monroe stabbed the wing, lifted it to his plate. "We need a guy who knows his way around the city and can pull a trigger if he needs to. Someone who's fearless enough to go out and collect money when it's slow coming in. We figure that a guy who's willing to shoot a man in a uniform might be good at this kind of work. You interested?"

Fearless? Me? "I want to talk to Earl Johnson."

His head snapped back at that. "What do you know about Earl?"

"Probably a hell of a lot more than you want me to know," I said. "Anyway, I know he's the one who makes the decisions."

He smiled again, and I hoped I'd made him think that I'd been looking into the group before the night at Southshore. "He's not here now. *I'm* making the offer."

I said, "How much of that hundred thousand a week do I get?"

Monroe laughed. "There's no hundred thousand. Not yet. That's what we're working toward."

"How much?" I said.

"An equal share of anything you're involved in."

I gestured at the cheap furniture. "No offense, but you're not exactly a poster boy for the riches you imply you're getting."

Monroe smiled like he was talking to someone of limited imagination. "I've got four years before mandatory retirement. Same thing for some of the other guys, give or take a couple years. Why would I do anything to call attention to myself? You know where I'm going in four years? Arizona—a little town outside Flagstaff. I've got the piece of property and I've got the architect plans. Slate floors. Redwood beams in all the rooms. Swimming pool. The works."

It sounded like his version of my little fishing village, but maybe he would have the money to buy the dream. I looked at Finley. I put him around thirty-five, more than twenty-five years away from Monroe's dream. "You already bankrolling your retirement too?"

He tilted his head and drained the last of a Heineken. "I'm not waiting for mandatory. I'm having fun along the way."

"Yeah?"

He exchanged glances with Raj.

"You want to see?"

I don't know if I nodded but the other three pushed their chairs back from the table.

"Let's go," said Monroe.

EIGHT

WE DROVE NORTH ON Michigan Avenue, Finley at the wheel, Monroe beside him, Raj in the back with me. The night was cold and windy. Shop windows glittered under the streetlights—jewelry stores, a high-end toy store, restaurants. When Michigan ended, we continued up the lakefront to a high-rise facing Oak Street Beach. Finley turned across the oncoming lane, drove the SUV onto the circular driveway in front of the building, and slowed to a stop.

A valet, who'd been standing under a heat lamp outside the building, jogged to the car and opened the doors. "Good evening, Mr. Monroe," he said, then greeted Raj and Finley by name. He nodded to me.

The big glass doors had brass handles and a doorman in gloves to use them. He also greeted Monroe, Finley, and Raj by name.

A large oriental rug covered most of the lobby floor. Leather sofas and easy chairs were arranged in a circle around a large dark-wood table. On the center of the table stood a tall vase with flowers and ferns fountaining out of the top. A crystal chandelier hung over the table. The room looked like a fine place to wait for a limousine.

A uniformed elevator operator stood by the elevator. He wished us a good evening. He didn't need to ask where to take us.

At the top floor, the elevator door opened to a lounge lighted by blue-tinted bulbs. A red neon sign hanging on the facing wall said THE SPA CLUB. About fifteen tables were scattered around the room, a third of them occupied, mostly by men who were drinking from highball glasses or eating small dinners off small plates. The waitresses wore high heels, short khaki skirts, and khaki halter tops like strippers who'd shopped at L.L.Bean. Behind a bar, two men in khaki safari shirts that hung tight over muscled bodies were making drinks in blenders.

"What is this place?" I said.

Monroe put a large hand on my shoulder and smiled. "It's where we hang out until we move to Arizona."

Raj said, "The mayor's been here."

Finley said, "Not the mayor himself. His chief assistant."

Raj nodded. "One of his chief assistants. And a lot of other guys you'd recognize."

Monroe said, "We run it. It's ours, you understand?"

A hostess approached, greeted us, and gave Finley a kiss on the cheek. Then Finley and Monroe left us, and the hostess led Raj and me to a table in the back of the room.

She asked us what we wanted to drink.

"Heineken," Raj said.

I said, "Bourbon."

Raj tilted his head and admired her as she walked away.

"What are we doing here?" I said.

He eyed me. "You've got a better place to be?" He leaned in. "You said you want to talk to Johnson. Johnson wants to talk to you too."

"Okay," I said, then asked again, "What is this place?"

He kept his face close to mine. "Private club."

"Uh-huh, I figured that much."

He glanced around the room at the waitstaff. "See anyone you like? You can have her." With his eyes on me again, he added, "Or him, if that's what you're into. We're equal opportunity. Or if you want, you can bring in a friend of your own and have a party with one of our staff. You can have whatever you dream of."

"You don't want to know my dreams."

Raj smiled and tipped his head toward a man and a woman at a nearby table. "See them?"

The man was tall and thin and had black hair and the pale, glistening, whiskerless facial skin that you sometimes see on burn victims. The woman was tall and thin too, flat-chested, with wheat-colored hair braided in pigtails. She had a bruise on her left cheek.

"He gave her the bruise," Raj said. "They're a perfect couple. He likes to hit her. She likes to get hit."

He glanced at a table of four men in their young thirties. Three had steak salads in front of them, one a piece of broiled fish. They wore blue jeans and shirts stretched tight over their biceps. "Wannabes," Raj said.

He nodded toward another couple.

She had black kinky hair that she wore tied back and eyes so weirdly intense you could see their blue across the room. He wore black pants and a black silk T-shirt. His gray hair was short, his beard at a couple days' stubble. He was no more than five foot four.

Raj said, "He's the most dangerous man in the place."

The woman kept her eyes on the short man when he spoke to her but when he looked down at his asparagus she gazed at the bartender, at me, at Raj.

Raj smiled at her.

She quickly turned away.

Raj said, "When a woman hangs out with a guy like him, she's always watching for her next move in case she needs out fast. I've seen it."

I started to feel sick the way you do when a whiskey drunk runs low, but I'd drunk plenty to keep going for another hour or two. I figured I was feeling the city and its rotting bodies, the ones rotting on the outside and the ones that looked like a hundred thousand dollars of plastic surgery on the outside but you knew the inside had gone bad.

Still, when a waitress brought our drinks, I tipped my glass back and downed the drink. It was top-shelf stuff, higher than I usually reached.

Across the room, a door opened behind the hostess station, and a man came out. He was wearing faded jeans and a heavy white cotton shirt. He moved with the ease of a man who owned everything around him. I hadn't seen Earl Johnson in six or seven years but had no trouble recognizing him. He looked the same as when we went through the academy together in the 1980s. Some guys get lucky that way naturally. Some work hard at the weights, diets, and the pharmacy to stay lucky. I figured he was a natural.

The woman with the black kinky hair and intense eyes

watched him as he crossed to our table, and she didn't turn away when he flashed her a smile.

He flashed me the smile too as he sat at the table. "Joe," he said with the warmth of an old friend. "It's been a long time. Life treating you well?"

I turned to Raj and said, "The last time I saw Earl, I was still in the department but barely. Then I lost the job, cleaned myself up, got married and divorced, played dad to my nephew, and opened a detective business that's kept my head above water most of the time. Now I've shot one of his friends and I'm drunk on his whiskey and mine. He knows damn well how life's treating me." Then I looked up at Johnson and said, "Couldn't be better," I said. "You?"

His smile held. "Can't complain. I'm keeping busy."

A waitress brought him a glass with a piece of lime and something clear in it. He hugged her around the waist. She gave him a smile and he let her go.

"You like this place?" he said.

I shrugged. "For an overpriced whorehouse, sure."

He ignored that. "My friends and I have worked hard to get where we are." The warmth dropped from his voice. "We're not going to let someone like you come in and fuck things up. You understand that, right?"

"I understand what you are."

He looked at me, patient. "You know, I'm a slow but steady learner. You and the other guys were way ahead of me in the academy. Everyone expected great things from you. Not me. I was a screwball. I'm sure you remember that. But I got through and I kept learning afterward. And now here I am, and there you are. Ironic, right?"

"I guess so."

He stared hard at me. "Kind of sad too."

"I suppose so. An honest jerk like me sitting at the table of an evil jerk like you—you'd think there's no justice."

He hit the table with his fist. The others in the lounge looked at him for a moment, then went back to their conversations. He spoke quietly. "Why did you meet with Bill Gubman this afternoon?"

"I already told your friends. Ask them." I pointed my thumb at Raj. "Ask *him*."

"I'm asking you."

I said, "Bill and I go back as far as you and I do. But I respect and like him."

"What did you tell him?"

I looked Johnson in the eyes and said, "I gave it all to him. I named you and Raj and the others. I gave him the dates and locations where you've boosted copper and appliances. I told him you're running prostitutes and said where. I told him you've got plans to poke your sticky fingers into all the corners of the city. What do you think I told him?"

Johnson sighed. "Did you give him any of our names?"

"If I told Gubman an eighth of what I know about you, you would be in jail, not sitting in your fancy club pinching your waitresses. No, I didn't give him your names."

Johnson said, "Why not?"

"I don't know," I said and kept spinning the story. "I guess I'm tired of being fucked over."

Johnson rubbed his fingers on his chin, eyed me. "I don't trust you," he said.

"Then you did learn something in all those years since the academy."

Johnson shook his head and laughed liked he figured I was an idiot. Then he stood. "I'm watching you."

I shrugged and lied again. "An eighth of what I know could bring you down."

He shrugged too. "Just as long as it doesn't." He crossed the room and disappeared back through the door he'd come out of.

Raj whistled low. "Earl's a dangerous guy to play with."

"Yeah," I said, "but he knows I can outplay him."

Raj laughed like he figured the whiskey had me thinking I was tougher than I was but he leaned in and said, "Okay, my honest man, are you going to work with us?"

"I don't think Johnson would like that."

Raj grinned. "He left the table without shooting you. And he said he's keeping an eye on you. That's as good as a job offer."

"I don't work well with others," I said.

"Finley's worked out the numbers. He figures each of us should clear ten thousand a month. That's for starters."

I stared at him.

He said, "Are you expecting a paycheck from somewhere else?"

I shrugged. "Okay," I said.

"Yeah?"

I nodded. "I'm in."

RAJ SHOWED ME AROUND the club. Beyond the lounge, it was like an upscale exercise club, with carpeted floors, painted steel railings, and the smell of chlorine, but no exercise equipment.

A hallway took us to a lobby where men and women relaxed on sofas or stood talking, most of the women in the khaki uniforms.

The far wall had floor-to-ceiling windows that looked out over Lake Shore Drive, across the beach, and to the lake.

Along a side wall stood a counter, staffed by a short-haired, healthy-faced woman whose khaki top barely contained her. A sign behind the counter listed the services available at the club. tension relief (40 minutes), $400. sensual awakening (75 minutes), $650. gentleman of leisure (2 hours), $700. couples spa (3 hours), $869. his and hers (1 hour), $750. group (75 minutes), $350 per person. other services negotiable. videographer available.

Another hallway led to doors cracked open an inch or two and other doors shut tight. Raj showed me inside the unoccupied rooms. One had a marble floor and marble wall tiles, a crescent-shaped hot tub, and a large cushioned bench. Another had three massage tables arranged side by side. A third had a thin gray mattress on a cheap metal bed frame, a bare bulb hanging from the ceiling, and walls that needed paint. "Fulfill your dreams, whatever they are," said Raj.

A blond-haired woman came out of a closed door and shut it behind her. She was barefoot and wore a short green sundress, the kind of thing that would slip off her shoulders and then she would have on nothing at all.

At the end of the hall, there was an emergency exit. Just before it, Raj used a key to let us into another room. The walls were lined with television monitors showing what was happening in the occupied rooms. A pock-faced man who looked about sixty sat on a desk chair with his feet propped on another chair, watching without interest, like the screens were airing a slow-moving ballgame. Two larger screens, off to the side, took video feeds from street level—in front of the building and behind.

Raj pointed his thumb at the screens. "If we ever get raided, the club can convert to legal massages real fast."

When we finished the tour, Raj took me to another closed door. "Signing bonus," he said.

"What?"

"For joining us. Go inside."

I pointed my thumb at my chest. Me?

He nodded and said, "It's been a tough couple of days."

I waved away the offer. "That's all right," I said.

He smiled. "Come on. Her name is Tina."

I went in.

The girl was lying on a white sofa. She was Eastern European—Russian, maybe Ukrainian. Her skin was pale, almost translucent. Her face was oval, her eyes the lightest blue, her hair so blond it was almost white. She was thin and had a wisp of white pubic hair and small breasts with dark nipples. She looked maybe seventeen or eighteen.

"Hi," she said.

My voice caught in my throat. "Hi."

She rolled over and sat at the edge of the sofa. She held her hand toward me, inviting me.

I wanted her badly. I stood where I was. "How old are you?" I asked.

She gave me a look. "How old do you want me to be?"

"I don't—"

She got up and came to me, put her hands on my shoulders by my neck like she either planned to strangle me or wanted me to fuck her. She didn't try to strangle me.

I said. "I have a wife."

Her eyes narrowed and her lips got mischievous. "You don't have ring on your finger."

"I have an ex-wife."

She looked confused.

I said, "It's complicated."

"Yes, complicated," she agreed, and moved her hands from my shoulders to my chest, caressing down toward my belt.

I stopped her hands with mine, held them to my lips, kissed her fingers. "I'm sorry," I said.

She looked angry for a moment but it passed. "Your loss," she said, and turned to the door.

"Yeah, my loss," I said, but she was already gone.

NINE

I LIVED ON THE Northwest side in a house I bought after Corrine and I split up. I got there after midnight. My car tires crunched on the asphalt alley and I parked outside the garage, then crossed under an old elm tree to my back porch. An October storm had knocked the last leaves off the elm and now the branches hung bare in the moonlight.

I let myself in and flipped on the kitchen light. For the past three months, ever since moving in with me, my nephew Jason had run in and welcomed me home at the end of an afternoon. Even when I'd come in at midnight, he'd stumbled out of his room to say hello. But Corrine had picked him up for school on the morning after the Southshore shootings, and now he should be sleeping at my mom's house in the bed I used as a kid.

Still, I called his name. I couldn't help myself.

When Corrine picked him up, Jason had left a half-eaten bowl of Cheerios in the sink. The milk had dried and the Cheerios had glued together and made a cake more solid than anything else in my life at the moment.

I left the bowl and went to the shower, stripped, and cranked the faucet full throttle so the pins of water hurt. I needed the hurt, though I knew it wouldn't wash all the dirt off of me. I stood for awhile and took it, then soaped myself and let the steaming water rinse me. I closed my eyes. The Russian girl at The Spa Club flashed in my mind. I wanted her and knew I shouldn't have her. Sex at The Spa Club was a bit of Arizona for Bob Monroe, and I figured it would help me escape too for an hour or so. Two hours with the *Gentleman of Leisure* package. But then what? I would be back where I was, sweating in front of Corrine, trying to explain myself.

I knew I should run away from Johnson and his crew. If one of his helpers threatened Corrine, Jason, and my mom, then I should get them out of town and go with them. It wouldn't be easy but I could do it.

Still, I'd laid the groundwork for the lies Bill Gubman wanted me to build. Bob Monroe was interested in what I knew about Johnson. Now I could start hinting that Johnson was freelancing and keeping the profits for himself. I could fill in the details later—places, times, amounts. Bill Gubman said he had a list of them that Johnson would have no alibi for, and phony bank accounts too. I could make the lies convincing if I moved slow and kept my head straight. I could help Bill make Johnson's crew self-destruct quietly.

But why should I?

Bill said I could redeem myself. If I did, though, I would be back in the place I was trying to escape. There was nothing I liked about where I was.

Except for Corrine. She was in that place too and I still wanted her.

And Jason. He also was there.

I laughed out loud the way a guy who lives in a cage laughs, half crazy, half to keep from going crazier. Then I turned off the water. The heat and sting wouldn't cure me. The only thing I could do was make the cage my own, make it as comfortable as I could since I was going to have to live in it.

I climbed into bed and after awhile I slept. An hour later I startled awake, worried about Corrine and Jason. Mom could take care of herself, I figured. I told myself that Corrine had been okay without me before we met and after we divorced, and Jason was safe in bed at Mom's house. But I still couldn't sleep. So I pictured the Russian girl coming to me at The Spa Club, imagined her face, which hadn't hardened yet, her nickel-sized nipples, the tuft of pubic hair that rose from her like a breath of smoke. I thought of the sweetness she'd offered me.

Eventually I dreamed. I was sitting at my office desk looking for a letter. Just a piece of paper with words on it. But I knew in the dream that my life depended on my finding it. I checked the desk drawers, the file cabinets, the carpet under the desk. The letter was gone. I got frantic and looked for my gun instead, stuck my fingers into an empty holster, checked the desk and file cabinets, patted my pockets. Gone too. The phone started ringing. Like it was in front of me on the desk, but there was no phone on the desk. It rang and I knew everything depended on my hearing the voice on the other end.

I startled awake again.

The phone was ringing. The dim gray light of early morning filled my bedroom.

I looked for my desk. I had no desk in my bed. I pawed for the phone on the night table. "Yeah?" I said into it. Breathless.

"Thank God! You had me worried, Joe." The voice was relieved and angry.

"I'm okay, Mom. They let me out yesterday."

"I know they let you out yesterday. They had it on the news." All anger now. "Why didn't you call?"

Because I wasn't ready to hear her voice. "What time is it?" I said, then looked at the clock on the night table and saw for myself. 7:10 A.M. "Never mind. I just woke up."

Mom was silent for a moment. Then, "Have you been drinking?"

"No. I've been sleeping."

Again she went silent for a moment. "Are you all right?"

I lied. "Yeah. I'll need to work things out, but I'm okay."

"The news says you shot a police officer."

"He was shooting at other police officers."

"That's not what the news says."

"Then they've got it wrong."

She went silent again, like she was waiting for me to explain what happened. I had nothing to add.

She asked, "Why didn't you call when they let you out?"

"I'm sorry that I didn't," I said.

"You don't listen to the messages on your answering machine?"

"I came in late last night. What's happening?"

"You don't answer your cell phone?"

"The battery ran out."

"While you were in jail," she said.

"As a material witness."

"The news called you a *person of interest*."

"Again, they got it wrong. What's happening. Are you okay?"

"*I'm* fine. Jason's in the hospital."

I felt the world falling away from me. "What—?" The words

caught in my throat. Jason had lived with me ever since my cousin Alexi ran off with a guy from the Jacksonville Port Authority and her mother and mine decided that her eleven-year-old would benefit from being around a father figure, even one like me. Now I'd fooled myself into thinking he was safe. He was in the hospital while I was lulling myself to sleep with fantasies about a high-priced hooker.

"He's all right," Mom said. "They took out his appendix."

The fear lifted and I felt my body relax. Little things go wrong all the time. This was one of them, nothing more.

"He's been asking for you."

"I'll go see him today," I said.

"He would like that."

More silence.

"I'm sorry about all this," I said. "Do you need anything?"

"I can take care of myself," she said and I figured that was true. But then she added, "Anyway, some of your friends already came by and offered to help."

"What friends?"

"Relax. Men you know at the police department. Detectives."

"Did they give you their names?"

"They did more than that. They showed me their IDs. One was a black man a little older than you and much bigger. Bob something. The other was white but had a foreign name."

"Raj?" I said, figuring *Bob something* was Bob Monroe.

"It could have been," she said. "I'd just gotten back from the hospital. I invited them in for coffee and they said I should let them know if they could help. They were very kind."

"They're not friends of mine, Mom."

"No?" She sounded more disappointed than concerned.

"If they come back, don't answer the door. Don't talk to them. Call me."

"Will you be picking up your phone?"

"This is serious, Mom. These guys don't want to help."

"That's a shame," she said.

I agreed that it was.

"Joe?" she said.

"Yeah?"

"Maybe you should leave town for awhile."

"Yeah," I said and I almost smiled. "That sounds like a great idea. Maybe I'll do that."

Mom gave me Jason's room number at Children's Memorial and we hung up.

I got out of bed, went to the kitchen, and started a pot of coffee. While it dripped into the pot, I looked out the back door into the yard. The sky was heavy and gray with the kind of cold rainless clouds that sometimes covered Chicago for a week at a time in November. The elm branches hung in the windless air just like they did last night. The tree was the last of its kind in the neighborhood. All the other elms had died from a disease in the 1970s.

After awhile I made my way into the living room. The red display on the answering machine said I had fourteen messages. Someone loved me. That was something.

But I figured I should take care of business first. I picked up the phone and dialed Bill Gubman.

"Did you change your mind about helping out and rent a fishing boat?" he said when I told him who was calling.

"I was about to," I said, "but then I started partying with

my friends Earl Johnson and Bob Monroe and I forgot about fishing."

"You've met with them? Good work."

"I didn't find them. They found *me*."

"Good work anyway," he said. "I've got some things for you—bank receipts, police reports, photographs. All that you need to set up Johnson."

"They're watching me pretty close. I can't pick them up at the department."

He considered that for a moment. "There'll be a ceremony this morning at Daley Plaza for the officers who died at Southshore Village. I'll be there with a package for you."

"Not exactly a private meeting," I said. "Half the city will be there."

"So no one will be surprised that you and I are both there. Look for me near the stage. We'll find someplace to talk."

Last thing I wanted to do. "I'll see you there," I said.

I hung up and stared at the phone. Then I punched the button on the answering machine and the machine spoke to me. "Listen, you asshole . . ." the first message started. It was a crank call from someone who'd heard early that I was involved in the shootings at Southshore Village, someone who knew how to reach me, someone who told me that he'd take me apart, joint by joint. That meant the caller probably was a cop, maybe a friend of one of the cops who were wounded or killed. So much for love.

Corrine had called four times. She was worried. She'd tried to find out where the police had jailed me but no one was telling. She'd figured my lawyer should know what was happening, so she'd called Larry Weiss, but he'd hit the same walls.

The first three calls sounded more and more worried. What were they doing to me? In the fourth message, which she'd left last night, she said, "Call me," and hung up. Like Mom, she must've heard that I was out of jail and gotten angry because I didn't run to her first.

Three calls were from Mom, worried too, the first when she was taking Jason to the hospital, the next telling me that he was all right, the last wondering where I was now that the police had turned me loose.

The crank caller called twice more to let me know new ways he'd worked out to cause me pain.

Lucinda Juarez had left the rest of the messages. She'd been my informal partner for the last month and a half. She'd also fallen into my arms, or I'd fallen into hers—only for a night, but that night kept rippling like a stone in water. It had almost drowned me and Corrine and it still might. Her voice had no worry in it. She reported on her calls to Larry Weiss and to the police department, where she'd worked until she joined me. She still had friends in the department but they'd told her nothing about me. "Hope you're okay," she said like she figured I was.

I picked up the phone and dialed Corrine. Maybe she'd be available for breakfast. Or lunch. Or dinner. Or a lifetime. Her phone rang twice before someone knocked on my front door. I hung up.

Lucinda was standing on the front porch. She was small and compact but had a weight and a strength that always surprised me. She wore jeans and a leather jacket and rocked a little like she was cold.

"Hey," she said when I opened the door, eyeing me like she might find me in pieces.

"Hey," I said. "Come in."

I stood aside and she did.

"You okay?" she said.

I tried a smile. "Great," I said. "I'm coming off a four-day vacation."

Then it seemed that, without moving, she was in my arms kissing me and I was kissing her.

"Damn," I said when we breathed for a moment.

Her dark eyes locked with mine. "God damn," she said. Then she kissed me again.

TEN

AT 10:30, LUCINDA AND I drove downtown to Daley Plaza. The police had cordoned off the surrounding streets. We parked three blocks away and walked into a swarm of uniforms and spectators. News vans were broadcasting in front of City Hall.

"It looks like a party," I said.

"Yeah," said Lucinda, "except for the tears."

In the center of the plaza, a bunch of people sat on folding chairs on a temporary stage. The mayor was there, somber in a dark suit. The police superintendent, a thick-shouldered man with a graying crew cut, sat next to him. Detective Chroler, who'd taken me into custody after the Southshore shootings, sat a couple of chairs away from the superintendent.

Two women, each with young kids, sat in a line of chairs off to the side. Families of the dead and wounded, I figured.

The flags at the east end of the Plaza were at half-mast.

"I hate this," said Lucinda.

"Yeah, me too."

We made our way toward the stage.

"What good does it do those kids to have them up there?" she said.

I said nothing. I'd given her most of the details about Southshore, my vacation in jail, and my introduction to Earl Johnson's crew. The more she'd heard, the angrier she'd gotten—at the department, at Bill Gubman for dragging me into the mess, at me too, it seemed, though I'd left out the Russian girl at The Spa Club.

Bill Gubman sat in a wheelchair at the base of the stage, just where he'd said he would be. I shouldered through the crowd, Lucinda behind me.

I was about twenty feet away when Bill saw me, but he turned away hard and looked at the stage. I stopped. On the stage a woman dressed in a dark skirt and matching jacket stepped to the microphone, introduced herself as a police department community liaison, and thanked the crowd for coming to mourn the loss of three young police officers and celebrate their lives of service. Almost everyone in the crowd was watching her, but a half dozen men in suits and ties hovered nearby with the unmoving faces of plainclothes officers at work. Three of them kept their eyes on Bill. I thought that maybe one or two were watching me.

When the woman finished the introductions the mayor moved toward the microphone and Bill maneuvered his wheelchair around and started working slowly through the crowd. Lucinda and I waited thirty seconds, then started walking through the crowd too, cutting away from Bill but always staying within sight.

Bill reached the sidewalk, cut along the edge of Daley Plaza, went around a corner, and headed toward a red-and-white striped awning that looked like it should house a circus but sheltered the entrance to the Hotel Burnham. He turned his chair and went into the hotel lobby. Lucinda and I made sure no one was watching us and then went inside after him.

The lobby was two stories high and had carpet that looked like it could've been skinned from leopards, a lot of dark wood on the walls, and heavy art-deco chandeliers. Bill was a big man but the room seemed to swallow him as he waited in his wheelchair just inside the door.

As I stepped in, a half smile formed on his lips. When Lucinda stepped in after me, the smile broke. He glanced again at her and then at me. "What the hell is she doing here?"

Lucinda crossed her arms over her chest. "Good to see you, Bill."

Bill's lips cracked into a little smile again. "Yeah, good to see you too, Lucinda." Like he might mean it.

"That's better."

"Now, take a walk, will you?" he said to her.

Lucinda looked at me.

I shrugged.

"Screw yourselves, then," she said and she stepped back outside.

"Sweet girl. Why did you bring her?"

"We work together."

He shook his head. "Not on this you don't. We've already got three police officers dead and two wounded. I don't want her to get hurt."

"Me, on the other hand—"

"That's right, you on the other hand."

"What do you have for me?" I asked.

He pulled a manila envelope from his jacket. "Dates, times,

and places where thefts occurred, totaling a hundred sixty thousand dollars. Police reports verifying the thefts. Bank records showing deposits into accounts in Johnson's name." He said it without pleasure.

"Was Johnson really involved in any of it?" I said.

"Not a bit."

"You're right about Monroe," I said. "He'll kill Johnson when he finds out he's been cutting him out."

"That's the plan."

I shook my head. "Who was watching us at Daley Plaza?"

"They're not in the department," said Bill.

"FBI?"

"Could be. If they are, it's news to me."

"Why not invite them into the investigation?" I said.

He laughed. "The FBI? No thanks. They wouldn't approve of this kind of cleanup."

"Then I'm not getting involved if they're watching."

"You were involved the moment you pulled the trigger at Southshore."

"Then I'm not getting in deeper."

"Probably a good idea," he said and held out the envelope.

"You're a bastard," I said and took it.

He laughed. "If you decide you really want out, dump the envelope in the garbage. If you stay in, be careful how you use the documents. Monroe will kill you instead of Johnson if he figures out what you're up to."

"Why would I stay in with a sales job like that?"

He stared me in the eyes. "What's left of you if you quit?"

It was a good question—a hard one but good—and I figured there was love and worry in it. So I called him a bastard again, stuck the envelope inside my jacket, and left him there.

Lucinda was outside, leaning against the building, arms crossed to keep warm. We walked back toward Daley Plaza. Lucinda raised her eyebrows. "Well?"

"He's afraid you'll get hurt," I said.

"He's a bastard."

"That's what I told him. But he's *our* bastard."

At the Plaza, we listened to the mayor's speech from the back of the crowd. He was talking about good men and women who put the safety of the city above their own and about the sacrifices they and their families made every day and the bigger sacrifices that a few of them made on especially terrible days, sacrifices that could never be repaid. I glanced at the row of wives and children and wished that I hadn't.

We turned away as the mayor finished his comments and a bugle started playing sad and soulful.

"What else did Bill tell you?" Lucinda said.

I wondered if Bill was right. Lucinda could get hurt and maybe I should keep my mouth shut. But she would never forgive me if I did. "He gave me the papers I need to bring Johnson down."

"Let's see."

"In the car."

"Do you trust him?"

"He's my oldest friend. He's always been there for me."

"Except when you were drinking heavily."

"He came around on that when his wife started abusing."

"When it served his purposes. It seems to me more like you've always been there for *him*."

"Except when he got shot."

"You didn't shoot him, and you did everything you could to help him afterward. As far as I can tell, you saved his life."

"I'm not sure he sees it that way."

She shrugged. "He might have it wrong."

"He's the closest friend I've got."

We walked north a block, then east toward the parking garage. The cold wind blew a plastic bag across the street. The bag rose along the side of a building and danced in the air five stories up like a dirty angel.

"So how do you want to work this?" Lucinda said.

I considered the possibilities. "I'm meeting with Bob Monroe and Raj this afternoon," I said. "I'll start feeding them information in little bits. If it goes well, they'll want more. Can you see what you can find out about these guys? What trouble have they gotten into in the department and outside it? Who are their friends? Anyone with power? I don't want surprises."

We came to the corner of Wabash and Randolph and stopped for the light. An El train screeched on the tracks above Wabash. A city bus rushed along the curb. A white GMC van slowed to a stop in front of us.

Lucinda moved close so her shoulder touched my arm. I smiled at her. We had a plan. That was something.

Then footsteps approached from behind. Too fast.

I spun.

Three men were closing in on us.

I'd seen them before. Fifteen minutes earlier, they'd watched Bill and me at Daley Plaza.

Lucinda and I could have backed off the curb but the bus would have flattened us. We could have run north under the El tracks. We could have yelled for help.

We stood where we were.

The men grabbed us and threw us against the white van.

Lucinda rolled to the side and caught one of them in his throat with her elbow. He went down on the sidewalk. She turned to another and he backed away and pulled a chained badge out of his jacket. It said FBI.

Lucinda stopped. "Shit! Why didn't you say?"

The man she'd knocked down peeled himself off the pavement. He was short and thick, with brown hair parted on the left and combed neatly to the side. The back door of the van opened, and the man with the badge—taller, older, and with less hair than the one Lucinda had hit—said, "Get in!"

I said, "Not me." Lucinda looked at me as though she wondered if she should start swinging again.

The two agents who'd stayed on their feet came at us hard. The one with the badge took me and the other one, bigger, took Lucinda. It was over in about fifteen seconds and the one with the badge repeated himself. "Get in!"

We got in.

The back door slammed and the van pulled away from the curb. Vinyl benches lined the sides. Lucinda and I sat on one, the FBI agents on the other. The man Lucinda had knocked down touched the tender spot on his throat and glared at me like it was my fault.

The one who'd told us to get in showed me an open palm. "Give it to me."

"What?" I said.

"The envelope Gubman gave you."

"What envelope?"

He looked disgusted. "Don't make me take it from you."

I shook my head. "Only with a court order."

More disgust. "Jesus Christ!" He cocked a fist and shifted toward me.

"All right," I said and fished the envelope out of my coat. He handed it to a woman sitting in the front passenger seat. "Do we get to know your names?" I said.

He gave me a grim smile. "No."

"Great," said Lucinda.

"What do you want?" I asked.

"We want to know what you're doing."

"I've spent half my life trying to figure that out."

He pursed his lips. "The man you killed at Southshore was working with us."

Lucinda sighed. "Shit."

I said, "He was FBI?"

The man shook his head. "He was a cop. A bad one. But he was also an informant. He's gone and so is most of our investigation into Johnson's crew."

I looked down at the van floor. "You should've kept tighter control of him, told him not to point his gun at other cops if he got caught."

The man Lucinda knocked down said, "You should've kept your finger off your fucking trigger."

The lead man frowned at him. "So," the lead man asked again, reasonable and level, "what are you doing?"

I shrugged. "I'm trying to dig myself out."

The man with the sore throat said, "You're up to your fucking ears. You're not getting out."

The lead man leaned toward me. "What did Johnson and his people want from you last night?"

I considered telling him what Bill Gubman had asked me to do and what Bob Monroe, Raj, and Earl Johnson had asked me to do—telling it all. I said, "Like you, they wanted to know what I was doing."

"For an hour and a half at Bob Monroe's apartment and three hours at The Spa Club?"

"You're not always as obvious when you're watching as you were at Daley Plaza," I said.

"That's not an answer."

"No, it's not," I agreed, and I asked again, "What do you want from me?"

The lead man went silent for a moment like he was considering options. "We want you to report what you hear from Johnson's group," he said.

I almost laughed. "You want me to be your new informant?"

He nodded once. "In a word."

I needed no time to think about it. "No."

He looked unsurprised but asked, "May I know why not?"

Because, I thought, with Bill on one side and Johnson's crew on the other I already was juggling knives. I didn't need the FBI to toss in another. "You won't even tell me your name," I said. "Why should I trust you? I figure when Johnson's crew goes down, you might let them take me with them."

He didn't deny it. He smiled. "My partner said you're in up to your ears, but he's wrong. You're in way over your head."

I smiled too, like that's where I wanted to be.

"As for you," he said to Lucinda, "I'd keep away from this guy. He just blew his only chance."

Lucinda put her hand on my thigh, squeezed, and said nothing.

The van stopped and the back door opened. We'd driven in a circle and were where we'd started. The woman in front handed the manila envelope back to the lead man. He glanced at it and handed it to me.

We climbed out, the door slammed, and the van drove west for a block and disappeared around a corner.

Lucinda looked at me. "Why'd they let you go?"

I shook my head. "Why'd they give me Bill's envelope?"

"Maybe they want you to keep doing what you're doing."

"I don't know what I'm doing," I said.

She laughed uncertainly.

"I don't," I said.

"Come on," she said. We crossed the street and stepped into the cold shade of the parking garage.

My cell phone rang. Lucinda and I jumped. I flipped the phone open, said hello.

It was Raj. "Where the hell are you?" he said.

"Why?"

He backed off. "I saw you at Daley Plaza. Then you were gone."

I wondered what he'd seen. If he'd seen us following Bill out of the Plaza, that would be trouble. If he'd seen the FBI agents shadowing me, that would be more. "I got tired of the noise and left."

"Pretty woman you were hanging with. Does your ex-wife know about her?"

"What do you want, Raj?"

"Change of plans. Monroe wants to meet this morning."

"I'm not available."

"Ten thirty at The Spa Club."

"Sorry. I'll see you this afternoon."

He sounded annoyed. "You've got something more important?"

"Than seeing you? Yeah," I said. "I do."

ELEVEN

JASON HAD A FOURTH-FLOOR room in Children's Memorial on Fullerton. The IV stand had a sock puppet over the top bar. Stickers of Spider-Man, Bart Simpson, and other cartoon characters covered the sides of the monitors. Painters had striped the white walls with yellow, red, and blue. In a lounge at the end of the corridor, a television was set to the Cartoon Network. But under every smiling face, you knew there was pain.

When I went in, Jason was lying in a hospital bed adjusted a quarter off horizontal, like a deck chair positioned to take in the afternoon sun. The television in his room was tuned to an animal show called *Wild Rescues*, which was doing a segment on koala kidnapping.

A doctor was examining Jason.

Mom sat in a chair by the window.

Jason grinned when he saw me. He was a tall, skinny eleven-year-old, and he wore a blue-dotted hospital gown. As usual, he needed a haircut. Mom got up and came to me, gave me a long hug, whispered, "Joseph," like I was a wild kid who'd finally fallen asleep. She was pushing seventy but normally looked fifty-five. Today she looked eighty. I wondered if I was responsible.

Jason tried to sit up but the doctor, whose tag identified him as Elijah Abassi, said, "Whoa, not yet, young man."

I went to the bed and handed Jason a bag with an iPod in it. "To pass the time until they let you out of here," I said.

He plugged it into his ears. "Sounds like a singing pirate," he said.

"Tom Waits."

"Cool. Thanks."

Mom moved over to me and put her hand on my arm like she needed to touch me to make sure I was real and solid and safe. I knew how she felt. I put my arm around her shoulders and hugged her.

I asked the doctor, "How long until you spring him?"

The doctor shrugged. "Another day or two. Possibly three."

"For an appendectomy?"

"For a postoperative infection."

"What happened?"

"It's not unusual, especially when the appendicitis is as far advanced as it was in Jason. The antibiotics seem to have it under control now."

"How far advanced was it?"

Another shrug. "Another hour or two, the appendix would have ruptured."

I turned to Mom. "Why didn't you get him here earlier?"

Her face lost color and she moved away. "Don't—" Her anger surprised me. "You were in jail," she said. "Jason was upset. When he said his stomach hurt, I thought—" She broke off.

I realized that she'd been as scared for Jason as I was. "I understand," I said, as gentle as I could manage.

"No, you don't," she said. "You were in jail. I don't like the work you do but I say nothing. You make your own decisions. But you're also my boy and I worry. *My* stomach hurt." She turned to Jason. "And then this happened."

I went to her but she pulled into herself and glared. She said, "No," and walked out of the room.

Jason looked at me. "You screwed up."

"That's a first."

He laughed, then clutched his side. "Ow."

The doctor said, "When we release Jason, who will be caring for him?"

"My mom, at first," I said.

"Good." He followed Mom out of the room.

I pulled a chair to the side of Jason's bed and sat. "How're you feeling?" I said.

He gave me his grin. "I'm okay."

I figured that was a lie but I didn't push him on it.

"I'm sorry I wasn't here for you."

"It wasn't your fault." He said it like a question.

"No, it wasn't. But I'm sorry anyway."

He pushed himself onto his elbows, winced, lowered himself. "Are you going back to jail?"

I shook my head. "They had me as a witness so they could talk to me any time they wanted. I didn't do anything wrong."

"The news said you shot a policeman."

"The policeman was threatening to shoot at other policemen. I shot to stop him."

He looked unsure but said, "Good."

There was a gentle knock at the door—polite, the way you

knock when you know you're interrupting something but want to come in anyway.

Corrine stepped in. I'd never managed to call her but she came to me and gave me a quick kiss like I'd never made a bad move in my life. In the last couple of years she'd gotten thick in the hips, and her long black hair was streaked with gray. But I liked to look at her. She dropped a brown paper bag on Jason's bed and said to him in a fake whisper, "Dirty magazines. Don't tell your uncle."

Jason ripped open the bag. It held three magazines—*Games*, *Skateboarding*, and *Powerboat*. "I don't skateboard, but thanks," he said.

We sat and talked about the Chicago parks that would be best for skateboarding if he ever started. We debated which powerboats would be good for fishing if we happened to move to an ocean-side village south of the Florida border. After awhile, Jason closed his eyes and drifted to sleep.

Corrine and I sat some more and watched him breathe, then stood and slipped out of the room.

The corridor was white and gleaming and quiet. A red line was painted down the middle of the white tile floor for busy times when the staff needed to divide the corridor into lanes.

Mom was standing outside Jason's door with a cup of tea.

I touched Corrine's elbow and said, "Give me a minute, okay?"

Corrine walked to the nurses' station. Mom looked up at me and said, "I'm sorry."

"No," I said. "You were right. I was feeling bad that I wasn't here for Jason, so—"

"I know," she said.

"He's looking good. Thanks for taking care of him."

She smiled as if to say, What else would I do?

For a moment, we stood without talking. "I'm going to get a cup of coffee with Corrine," I said.

Mom nodded. "Tell me that you're innocent."

She knew I wasn't, not in the bigger sense. I said, "I'm innocent."

She said, "Is this over?"

I didn't like to lie to her. "Yeah, it's over," I said.

"Don't lie to me."

I said, "I'm trying to clean things up."

She looked at me long as though there might be something inside me that she'd missed. She said, "Your father was a policeman for twenty-seven years, and one thing I learned was that some things don't get clean. Some things it's better to walk away from."

I nodded. "You're a smart woman, Mom."

"Walk away."

"All right," I said. "I'll try to."

"It's not hard. People do it all the time."

CORRINE AND I RODE the elevator to the basement cafeteria, got coffee, and sat at a table. She had a calm look that I knew not to trust. She said, "Where the hell have you been?"

The cafeteria was empty except for two women in blue surgical scrubs and a man off in a corner reading a book. No one who would cause me trouble. So I told my story again, including my meeting with Bob Monroe and the memorial service at Daley Plaza, but leaving out the bottle of bourbon, The Spa Club, the Russian girl, and Lucinda.

Corrine sighed when I finished. "Yeah, you've got to fix this. You've got to make it right."

I felt a weight lift from me. "I do?"

She frowned and shrugged. "You can't just turn your back on it, can you?"

I leaned across the table and kissed her. "No, I can't," I said.

She sat back in her chair and cocked her head to the side. "Why didn't you call when you got out?"

"Sorry," I said.

"I know this is hard," she said, "but it can be hard with me or without me. With me, it might be a little easier."

I nodded.

"Tell me what you need."

I said, "I will."

She put her hand in mine. "I want you if you want me," she said.

"I want you."

She looked down at the table, then up at me. "Could we go somewhere for awhile?"

I said, "That would be good."

WE DROVE TO HER house and went up the front stairs. Until our divorce, her house had been our house, her bedroom ours. The rich smell of sleep in the bedsheets was still the same. The photographs on the wall—three black-and-white sixteen-by-twenties of staircases, the middle one with a woman on it—were the same too. Corrine had brought the photographs into our house and had kept them when I moved out. The other pictures that we'd had, framed photos of the two of us together, were long gone, into storage or out with the trash. She'd bought new night tables. I wondered how many other men she'd brought home to her bed.

Then she came to me and we kissed and I stopped wondering. She pulled her mouth from mine and unbuttoned my shirt, stripped it off my shoulders. I unbuttoned her blouse and let it fall. She kissed my chest, ran her fingers over me, scraped my nipples with her fingernails.

"What are you doing?" I whispered.

She put her mouth on me again, nibbled, and answered, "Biting you."

She nibbled some more. I whispered, "Why?"

"It will feel good." She bit harder.

"Ouch."

"Relax—"

"Ouch!"

She pulled away. "I don't think you're giving this a chance."

I lifted her face to mine, kissed her, and said, "I'll give you a chance."

I did.

We did.

Twice.

TWELVE

AT 2:30 IN THE afternoon I drove back to The Spa Club. The valet in front of the building was new and didn't recognize me, but when I told him my name and said I was there to see Bob Monroe he tipped his head respectfully, opened my door, and said he would park my Skylark in front so it would be available when I needed it.

I fished a five-dollar bill from my wallet but he said, "Not necessary, sir."

I eyed him. "Do you curtsy?"

He said, "I do anything Mr. Johnson and Mr. Monroe pay me to, sir."

I rode the elevator to The Spa Club.

The lounge outside the elevator door was empty except for a table where a fat man in a white shirt and dark tie was eating a late lunch. A new hostess stood at the desk. She smiled and looked me up and down like she was measuring me for a new suit or a bed. So I looked her up and down, the same, and said, "I'm here to see—"

"Mr. Monroe," she said, still with the smile. She tilted her head toward the private hallway that extended from behind the desk. "He's in Mr. Johnson's office. Through the hall, the door on the right."

"It's good to be recognized," I said.

A door on the left was open to an office with a desk and computer. The door on the right was closed. When I raised my hand to knock, it swung open and the Russian girl stumbled out. Raj had called her Tina when he'd offered her to me. She wore a man's shirt, yellow, unbuttoned except at the bottom, and nothing else. She had glazed eyes and her lips were bent between a grin and pain. She brushed past me like she'd never seen me before.

"Tina?" I said.

Nothing. Not a twitch.

I knocked.

The door swung open again.

I recognized the man who opened it. He'd loaded a spool of copper wire into a van at Southshore Village just before the shooting started.

"Hey, come on in," he said.

This office was four times the size of the one across the hall. It had a brown leather couch, a brown leather chair, an Oriental carpet between them, and a large dark-wood desk, also with a leather chair.

Bob Monroe sat in the desk chair, Raj sat in the other chair, and the man who'd opened the door joined another guy from the Southshore robbery on the couch. They were having a party.

Monroe looked me over. "You're sober today." Like that surprised and didn't completely please him.

"True."

"Want a drink?"

"I always want a drink."

"Bourbon?"

I nodded.

He picked up the telephone, punched a button, and said, "A Heineken, a couple shots of Maker's Mark, and a glass of water."

When he hung up, he leaned forward and said, "Ready to get started?"

"Sure."

"We're holding an organizational meeting tonight. Representatives from twelve of the city's gangs will be there—El Rukns, Latin Kings, Black Gangster Disciples, La Raza, Vice Lords, and a bunch of others. The Asians have refused to participate but they'll come around. We're not bothering with the small gangs at this point."

"Where's the meeting?"

He ignored the question. "Earl will do the talking and the rest of us will be there. Rules are, no weapons, no flashing signs, and no more than two representatives from each gang. We wanted just one but some of them said they wouldn't come alone. As much as possible, everyone drives in on separate streets. If we all play by the rules, the meeting should go fine. But these guys never saw a rule they didn't break. Your job and mine will be to make sure no one gets shot and no one gets in a fight that spills back into the neighborhoods. Earl's job will be to tell the gang representatives what we expect them to do and what they can expect in return. They keep violence to a minimum and cough up their money, and we let things slide when we can. We make money and they make money. They stay alive and out of jail and we make more money."

"Who could object?" I said. "Will *we* have guns?"

"Officially, no. But we'll stash a couple in the room just in case."

"Why not meet with the gangs separately?" I asked. "Seems like it would be a lot safer and easier."

He shook his head. "We need to set an example of what happens if the gangs don't pay. We don't want to have to set twelve separate examples."

Raj said, "That would be too much blood, too much anger."

I said, "What are you planning to do?"

Monroe shrugged like it was no big deal. "Just enough to scare the fuck out of them."

I didn't like any of it. "Where's the meeting?"

"Neutral ground. Raj will pick you up at your office at eight."

Fingers tapped at the office door and Tina came in, still in the yellow shirt, carrying a drink tray. She put a highball glass, half full of whiskey, and a glass of water on a table next to me, then took the bottle of Heineken to Monroe.

He reached under her shirt and put his hand on her ass. "Thanks, Tina."

I drank about an ounce of bourbon off the top. When the first burn faded, I said, "Do I also get a cut of the copper sales?"

Monroe tilted his Heineken over his mouth and drank a third of it. "You get a cut of anything you put your hands on."

"Good."

"Next time we find a place with enough metal, we'll arrange something."

I said, "How about the warehouses? They seem like more money for less work."

Monroe looked confused. "What warehouses?"

Bill Gubman's papers included false information about robberies that Earl Johnson supposedly committed at three ware-houses. I drank more bourbon, then named two of them, as if to catch him in a lie. "Thompson Metals on Elston? National Brass and Copper on California? I was looking into you guys long be-fore Southshore. I've probably got better records of what you've been up to than you do."

"I don't know what you're talking about."

Of course he didn't. I put anger into my voice. "Don't try to cut me out—"

He patted the air. "Take it easy," he said. He grinned, like all was good in the world. "So you've kept records on us?"

I grinned too. "Records, pictures, numbers."

"And you haven't given them to your Southshore client?"

"Ex-client," I said. "No."

He looked happy at that. "Pictures at the warehouses?"

"Sure."

"Who's in them?"

I shrugged. I needed him to work to bring down Earl John-son.

He said, "Well, it sounds like we need to be more careful about who's watching."

The office door swung open again and Johnson came in. He scowled when he saw Monroe at the desk and me talking with him, but he caught himself. "Good afternoon, gentlemen." Then to me, "I didn't expect to see you back so soon."

Monroe said, "I've asked him to come to the meeting to-night."

Anger flashed across Johnson's face. "Why the hell did you do that?"

Monroe looked at him level, a big man comfortable in his skin. "After Southshore, we're short numbered. Raj and I talked about it. Anyone acts up tonight, it'll be good to have another man on our side."

Johnson's voice dropped low in disbelief. "You and Raj talked about it?"

Level. "Yes."

"And where the fuck was I?"

"We didn't know where the fuck you were. That happens a lot lately. We don't know where the fuck you are."

"I'm out covering your ass while you're here making stupid decisions," Johnson said. He crossed behind the desk and stood near Monroe. Monroe was sitting in his desk chair. For a moment, Monroe stayed where he was as if Johnson might go away. When he didn't, Monroe stood and moved easily around the front of the desk. Johnson sat in the chair. He gestured at me. "Who's this guy other than he killed Dave? Why should I trust him? Why should you?"

Monroe was wearing an untucked black silk shirt that hung over black pants. He was a big man, and when he sat on the corner of the desk he was the most impressive man in the room. He said, "Joe's got nothing to gain by working against us and everything to gain by working with us. Also, he's good at what he does."

"Yeah?" said Johnson. "Like how?"

"Like he was just telling me about his investigation into us before Southshore. Says he kept records." Monroe was casual but he kept his eyes on Johnson. "Says he has pictures of us at the construction sites. Other pictures too. What did you say they were? Thompson Metals and National Brass and Copper?"

I nodded.

If you weren't looking close you might've missed Johnson

flinching at the mention of the warehouses. But I was looking close. So was Monroe.

Then Johnson glanced away like I was a minor distraction. "Now that you're involved with us, you might want to burn the photos."

I looked at him. "Am I going tonight?"

He looked back. He was barely tolerating me. "Sure. If it turns out you're fucking with us, we'll turn the gang reps loose on you. They'll tear you apart."

THIRTEEN

YOU CAN'T BUY A gun legally in Chicago. You've got to drive into the tree-lined suburban streets. There, between a dry cleaner and a 7-Eleven, you can get a SIG SAUER pistol with a night sight or an M16, anything short of a rocket launcher.

But Theo's Pawn and Coin in the southwest Loop kept a small stock under the counter. If the owner knew you, she would sell you something from her illegal collection. She had few choices but she kept the guns well oiled and clean.

I stopped by Theo's on my way to my office.

Theo died in the early 1990s and his wife Susie ran the store. She was a tough, short, wide-faced woman in her fifties with flat brown hair that she kept in a ponytail. She wore short-sleeved T-shirts year round. A large tattoo peaked from under her right sleeve. The tattoo said *Love* in large looping letters. The rumor was she'd killed Theo to get the store.

"Joe!" She grinned as I came in. "Long time."

A dozen acoustic guitars hung on the wall behind her. Next to them were three violins, a banjo, a drum set, and a stack of stereo tuners. Power tools hung in the front window. A long glass case held jewelry, cameras, and watches. A sign on the wall said, *merchandise sold as is. no returns, no refunds. cash only. checks accepted. deposits not refundable. have a nice day.*

I was the only customer in the store, which made my life easier.

I went to the counter and Susie leaned against it on her elbows. She looked in my eyes like an old lover.

"What can I do for you?" she said.

"I need a gun."

She frowned. "I was afraid you'd say that. You know I can't help you. You're on TV, and I don't sell high-risk. The cops find a gun on you and trace it to me, and I've got to go into early retirement."

"I'll pay twice what you're asking."

She rolled her eyes. "Jesus! Do you think I'm that easy?"

"Yeah, usually. I'll pay whatever you're asking."

"Wow," she said and she looked at me, worried. "You're hungry for a gun."

I admitted I was.

"You know, if you find yourself a girl for a night, that can sometimes take care of the itch, and it's a lot less dangerous."

"I'm not planning to shoot anyone. I'm trying to keep from getting shot."

She stared at me awhile and then flipped a wall switch behind the counter. I'd seen her flip that switch before. It automatically locked the front door. Anyone who wanted to come in now would need to hit a buzzer.

She reached under the counter and removed a small Ruger .38 semiautomatic. The grip had some wear but the gun looked like it would shoot just fine.

"It holds six, plus one," Susie said. "I'll charge you three-fifty. I could ask for more."

"You got anything else?"

She looked irritated. "Take it or leave it."

"I'll take it. And a box of fifty rounds."

I paid cash, which she slipped into a pocket in her jeans. She slid the gun into a soft case and handed it to me. "Happy shooting," she said. "Or not."

"Thanks, Susie."

I turned to go.

"You sure you don't need a girl?" she said.

I turned back. "I've got all I can handle right now."

She leaned on the counter. "Tell."

I smiled at her. "Another time."

LUCINDA HAD LET HERSELF into my office. When I walked in, she was sitting at the desk, working at the computer.

She'd set my mostly empty bottle of Jim Beam at the edge of the desk to make it conspicuous. She'd also fished through the desk drawers. The Baggie of cocaine was propped against the bottle.

It was an accusation.

I went to the bottle, unscrewed the cap, and took a drink. The Baggie fell to the floor and I left it there.

"You bastard," she said without looking up from the computer.

I drank again.

She said, "I don't work with drunks or cokeheads."

"Good policy." I took another drink.

She spun from the computer, her eyes full of fire. "What's wrong with you?"

"Where do I start? I shot a cop because I figured that if I didn't he'd kill some innocent men. Then the innocent men threw me in jail for three days. For trying to save them, I guess. When they let me out they convinced me to join up with the guys who were shooting at them. Why would anything be wrong?"

She shook her head, disgusted. "Since when did you start feeling sorry for yourself?"

"I've always felt sorry for myself!" I said.

She looked at me long. Then she laughed. When she caught her breath, she said, "You're hysterical."

I drank. "See? No sympathy."

She nodded at the bottle. "You keep that up, you're going to sleep tonight facedown on the floor."

I thought about that and thought about my evening plans with Earl Johnson's crew and Chicago's gangs. I screwed the cap onto the bottle. "You're probably right." I dropped the bottle in the trash can.

Lucinda's eyes were doubtful. "Really?"

I shrugged. "If the cleaning service doesn't empty the garbage tonight, I'll probably dig it out tomorrow."

That seemed enough for Lucinda, or almost. "What about the coke?"

I picked the Baggie off the floor. "You want it?"

She shook her head no.

I dropped it in the garbage on top of the whiskey bottle, though it felt like lighting a fire in front of an exit door.

She sighed. "Now tell me what's up."

I filled her in on the meeting I'd agreed to attend and the

illegal Ruger I was carrying even though the rules were against bringing guns. When I finished, she glanced at the garbage can like she might need a drink.

"You want me to tail you?" she said.

I shook my head. "Too dangerous. Johnson and his crew are going to be watching. If they see you in the rearview mirror they might get the idea that La Raza or the Latin Kings are making their own plans for the meeting."

"You going to tell Bill Gubman about this?"

"I wasn't going to. You think I should?"

"I don't think you should get in a car with Johnson's guys and go hang out with gangbangers unless you've got backup."

"Bill would want to do the same thing as you—tail me. I think I'm safer without that."

She looked unhappy but said, "Okay."

"What have you found?" I asked.

"A lot. Some of it interesting." She picked up a stack of paper from the computer printer. "Earl Johnson finished third from the bottom of the same academy class you were in. You finished third from the top. Nice symmetry."

"That's on Google?"

She shook her head. "I called records. Johnson's gotten four commendations and two complaints. Nothing unusual for a vice detective. Most of the other guys have records that look about the same."

"What were the complaints for?"

"First, a hooker says he made an agreement with her—she has sex with him and he doesn't arrest her. She says they did it a couple of times. But then he took her money and arrested her anyway. Internal affairs investigates but the hooker disappears. Complaint file is closed. Second, a pimp says Johnson beat him up and took his money. Internal affairs investigates again but the pimp disappears too. Complaint file closed."

"Yeah, that sounds like Johnson."

"The commendations are all from good citizens whose neighborhoods he cleared of prostitutes. Bob Monroe's record on vice is shorter, one complaint and one commendation. He came over from the gang unit two years ago. His gang record is clean—officially—but I made another call and the word is he got too friendly with some of the guys he was supposed to be policing. It never went to internal affairs but that's why they moved him to vice."

"Who told you that?"

"I've still got friends in the department. A couple of them anyway."

I told her about Victor Lopez, the kid Bill Gubman told me about, who had complained about Monroe and then vanished and was presumed dead. Then I asked, "What else?"

She leafed through her papers, pulled out a few sheets. "The one I can't figure out is Raj. He's basically an eagle scout. Six service commendations. No complaints. Fast track to detective. Unless there's another Farid el Raj in Chicago, he also coaches his son's Little League team and is a member of the Lebanese-American league, serving as Chicago-area chairman of philanthropic outreach. What's he doing with Johnson and Monroe?"

I shrugged. "Greed is greed. He looks happy enough when he's at The Spa Club."

"I Googled the club name and got hits for a chain of spas in Utah and a stand-alone in Minnesota—straight places, unrelated to Johnson's. Johnson's club doesn't appear at all, not even on the adult chat boards."

"It's not like they're advertising next to the escort services."

"Yeah, but it's hard to keep quiet about a place like that," she said. "Sooner or later, some guy's going to boast about getting laid, even if he paid a thousand dollars for it."

"The guys who run The Spa Club have a lot of incentive to keep the place a secret. The people who go there have a lot to lose too. If they slip and it comes out, they fall hard."

Lucinda gave me a half smile.

"What?" I said.

"I think I see them slipping."

A little after 6:00, we walked out and had dinner at a Chinese restaurant called Opera, which made the best garlic black bean shrimp in the city. We split an order of the shrimp, some Hainanese mussels, and the black tiger prawn Singapore noodles. For an hour, the city seemed far away. Outside the window, the November wind sucked away the last warmth and life from the leafless branches of the trees in the curbside planters. It swung the metal and plastic sign that hung over the door of the bank across the street. Yellow cabs shined their headlights into the back windows of other yellow cabs as they took their passengers to whatever happiness or sadness was waiting for them at home. But inside the restaurant, the air was warm and smelled of garlic and chili peppers, and the light was low and comforting. A waiter brought a pot of tea, then plate after plate of hot food. He said to let him know if there was anything else he could bring us. It would be his pleasure to bring it, he said. Like we deserved it.

Afterward, we stood outside my building. Lucinda looked at me close. "Be careful tonight," she said.

I nodded.

She moved in closer. "Give me a call when you get back."

"It'll be late," I said.

She nodded. "Give me a call."

"Okay."

She looked at me with her dark eyes. She was wearing jeans and a brown leather coat that she'd zipped up to her chin. She looked small and warm and self-contained.

Already I felt the cold wind seeping into my skin.

She leaned onto her toes and gave me a quick kiss on the lips. Then she was gone.

I rode the elevator to the eighth floor. During the day, the hallway would fill with students from the secretarial school. Roselle Turner cashed the students' federal loan checks and sank a few pennies from each of them back into the school. Half of the computers were broken and the other half were ten years old. Still, the students dressed up for school each day and you could hear the hope in their voices.

Now the hallway was silent, the classroom lights off.

I let myself into my office and went straight to the garbage can. I took out the Baggie and the bottle, put them in a file cabinet drawer, and locked it. No telling when Lucinda would poke around again.

Then I sat in my desk chair.

The steam radiator clanked twice and went silent. Traffic passed on the street below with a hush as soft as waves breaking on a distant beach. A car horn honked far away.

I turned the chair to the window and sat with my feet on the sill. In a lighted window of the insurance building across the street two men were arguing. In another window, a cleaning woman mopped a floor with her eyes turned downward. Most of the other offices were empty.

I swung the chair back to my desk and loaded the Ruger. *Be careful*, Lucinda had said. Good advice.

What were the dangers?

The police department was like a small town when it came to secrets. Sooner or later Johnson would learn that I was working with Bill Gubman. He already knew I was Bill's friend. Unless he was sloppier than he looked, he would already be asking questions. His crew couldn't have lasted a month unless he knew people in the department who would give him answers. What would he do when he found out I was helping Bill set him up to take a fall? Putting a bullet in my head might seem like a justifiable defense. Throw Chicago's street gangs into the mix and I had another dozen angles to protect. Whatever else Johnson and his crew called their scheme, they were extorting the gangs. Taking a few bucks a week from each member sounded harmless until you did the multiplication. When Johnson introduced me as a money collector, the gang members would see me as an enemy and they had a long history of killing enemies.

At 7:40, I went back to the file cabinet where I'd stashed the bourbon and cocaine and unlocked it. Another drawer held shorts, a T-shirt, and a pair of running shoes—for mornings when I had time to jog through Grant Park—and a pair of baggy black pants and a black Windbreaker, for nights when I needed to be invisible. Under the clothes were a small toolbox, a ball of twine, and a roll of duct tape. I took out the pants and tape and re-locked the cabinet.

I stripped off my jeans, taped the gun to my inner thigh, and put on the black pants. Reaching the gun would take some work, but most body searches stick to the outside of the legs. Ripping off the tape might sting but not as bad as taking a bullet.

I went out to the men's room that I shared with the secretarial school and splashed cold water on my face in the sink. The eyes that stared back at me in the mirror looked tired and scared. I tried to flatten my emotions, make my face say nothing. Corrine used to say that I looked like Lech Walesa from Poland's Solidarity days, but forget the moustache. Maybe if I grew the moustache I could pull off a cool Eastern European look.

I went back to my office and stared across the street at the insurance building. The arguing men were gone. So was the cleaning woman. The building was a slab of concrete and glass, like a monument to the people who spent their lives there.

At 8:03 the phone rang. Raj was waiting in a car outside the building. I told him I would be right down.

FOURTEEN

WE DROVE WEST FROM my office in Raj's SUV. He put a
Cal Tjader CD on the stereo and tapped the steering wheel to
the beat. He glanced at the rearview mirror, back to the street,
and at the mirror again.

"Someone following us?" I asked.

He glanced again, then cut hard to the left, crossed the oncoming traffic, and shot down South Clark Street. At the corner, he stopped and looked at the mirror. "No," he said.

We turned right and, a block later, right again. At Congress
Parkway, we stopped at another stoplight. Raj flipped on his
left-turn signal and I glanced over my shoulder.

A white GMC van pulled close behind us.

Even in the dark, I recognized the men in the front seat—
the lead FBI agent who'd stopped me and Lucinda after we left
the Daley Plaza memorial service, and the man Lucinda had
elbowed in the throat. The van had on its left-turn signal too.

When the stoplight turned and Raj pulled into the intersection, I said, "Go straight."

He gave me a look.

"A van's following us."

He continued straight across the intersection and glanced in the mirror.

"Fuck," he said and accelerated.

"They're following me, not you," I said.

He turned left at the next corner as a light turned red. After three cars passed, the FBI agents got a chance and the van ran the light and fell in behind us.

"They stopped me earlier," I said. "They're investigating the Southshore shooting. David Russo's the second cop in a couple of months to get shot when I was around. They don't like the coincidence."

We sped west for four blocks. The van dropped back, couldn't get around the cars in front of it.

Raj swung around the corner onto Upper Wacker. "Who are they?" he said.

"FBI."

"Fuck. You tell Monroe or Johnson about them?"

I hung onto the overhead handle as we accelerated. "Not yet."

"Why not?"

"When the FBI figures out that there's nothing behind the police shootings but coincidence, they'll leave me alone."

He gripped the steering wheel in both hands, leaned over it. "Meantime, you put the rest of us at risk."

We flew north and pulled a U-turn, went down a ramp into the orange light of Lower Wacker. We were doubling back toward Congress. Steel I beams supported the street over our heads. Steel pillars on the sides and in the medians supported the I beams. It was a lot of metal that could impale us a hundred different ways as we sped past. At Congress, we bounced up an exit ramp and merged into traffic.

Raj looked in the rearview mirror. I looked over my shoulder.

The white van was gone.

Raj breathed in deep and sighed. "Thanks for telling me they were behind us."

I let go of the overhead handle and felt blood return to my fingers. "Anytime."

We continued to the Kennedy Expressway and turned onto the on-ramp, heading north toward the suburbs and the Wisconsin border. Raj relaxed, steering with one hand, weaving past slower cars. He gave me a quick look. "Let's keep the FBI to ourselves, okay?"

"Yeah?"

"Johnson already doubts you. If he hears about this, you're done."

"How about you? You doubt me?"

Another look. "Should I?"

I shrugged. "Probably. But no more than you should doubt the rest of the guys. How about Monroe? What's he think of me?"

He spoke to the windshield. "He figures you've got more to gain and less to lose than any of the rest of us."

I thought about what Lucinda had found out about Raj. The records she'd seen made him look as clean as an eagle scout. It seemed *he* had the most to lose. "What about you? What do you get out of this?"

His face darkened and he said nothing. Then, still to the windshield, he said, "I've got responsibilities."

"Yeah?"

Again silence. Then, "Big family."

"How many kids?"

He shook his head. "Just a son. But my mother's in Lebanon. I send her money. And my sister and her family. She's got four kids. And my cousins. Too many cousins."

I nodded. "Nothing in life is free."

He smiled again. "It sure as hell ain't."

We drove for awhile, quiet.

"How about your wife?" I said. "She also Lebanese?"

He laughed. "Irish Catholic."

"Yeah?"

"Yeah. And from what I understand, you've got an ex-wife who you're still seeing and a partner who you're sleeping with."

That stung. "Where'd you hear that?"

He glanced at me like that was a dumb question. "We've asked around."

"Well, I'm working things out."

He nodded. "It's a fucked-up world."

That made me grin. "Yeah, it is."

FIFTEEN

WE DROVE NORTH FOR an hour through suburbs with lakefront mansions, then onto a dirty strip of highway lined with dimly lighted signs for auto body shops, tire dealers, and trucker motels. Eventually the businesses were replaced by farms. Before the state line, we passed another lighted sign, for the Mount Rest Cemetery. Then a billboard welcoming us to Wisconsin loomed up on the roadside and we drove on in the dark.

A few miles later, we got off the highway and rode through an industrial strip at the edge of a town called Pleasant Prairie. We took some more turns and suddenly, even with the windows closed, the air felt cold and damp and smelled of pine. We were near Lake Michigan. An asphalt road led us past houses and cottages and, as we came around a bend, past a strip of beach where the whitecaps on the lake appeared and disappeared in the headlights. A couple minutes later, we arrived at a lone house surrounded by trees at the end of a gravel driveway. Raj turned the wheel and we went in.

A Mercedes SUV, a rusted Chrysler LeBaron, and about a dozen other cars lined the driveway. The house was bright, inside and out. Spotlights rigged to tree branches with extension cords threw an orange glow and long shadows over the yard. As we parked, two men got out of a nearby car and started toward the house. They wore loose blue pants, black high-tops, and nylon Windbreakers. One had a black skullcap with a Nike swoosh. The other had shaved his head clean and had a tattoo that said STREET in block letters on the back of his neck.

Another car pulled next to us, windows tinted, music pounding. The bass beat made the dashboard rattle in the SUV.

"Ready?" Raj asked.

The duct tape holding my gun to the inside of my thigh pinched my skin. "Ready," I said.

We got out and walked to the house. It was a big log cabin, the kind you can have designed and built by a company that does nothing else. I figured the side facing the lake would have big windows and a wood deck with a Weber grill on it.

"Whose place is this?" I said.

"Peter Finley's. He calls it a fishing lodge, but mostly he comes up here and gets drunk."

On the front porch, Finley and another cop I recognized from the Southshore construction site were checking for guns while a little crowd of guys who I figured were gang members watched. Raj stepped up to the other cop and raised his hands. The gang members laughed while the cop frisked him. "Feel him good," said one of them.

I stepped up to Finley and raised my hands. He swept the tops and bottoms of my arms with his fingers, traced my ribs, back and front, and ran his hands down the outside of my legs.

Then he brushed the inside of my legs. He barely paused when he touched the Ruger, but he looked at my eyes.

I stared at him, silent.

"Of course," he said. He turned to the guys who'd arrived in the car with pounding music. "Next."

Inside, the house had been designed with an open floor plan. The walls were knotted pine paneling, the ceiling too. Framed prints of deer and moose hung on the walls. There were a lot of chairs and sofas and at one end of the room a large stone fireplace with a wide hearth. In the kitchen, two refrigerators stood side by side with enough space to hold a dozen cases of beer and as much trout as Finley could catch. The wall facing the lake was all windows. Outside the windows, lighted with more spotlights, was a wood deck with a Weber grill on it.

The living room was crowded with gang members, mostly in pairs, along with Johnson's crew. There were a lot of tattoos, plenty of cornrows and shaved heads, some skullcaps, baseball caps, and bandanas. A couple of guys wore sunglasses, though the sun wouldn't shine for another ten hours. They drank from cans of beer that they'd taken from a big bin of ice on the floor in the center of the room. Everyone was quiet, almost polite.

Earl Johnson stood by the fireplace and explained the deal. He wanted each gang to give him a list of active members. Then, each gang member would be responsible for paying ten dollars a week and in return Johnson and his crew and anyone else they had access to in the department would leave the gang members alone as long as things didn't get too out of hand. He said, "The first thing you're wondering is why you've got to give us a list of your names." Most of the gang reps nodded. "From our side of the bargain," he said, "it's simple business sense. If we don't have the names, we don't know if you're ripping us off. From your side, we'll know who to let slide. If your name's on the list and we catch you being a bad boy, we apologize for inconveniencing you. Meantime, we spend all the extra time we've got hassling your competition—the guys whose names aren't on your list."

He paused to let the gang reps think about the plan. The look in their eyes said most of them bought it or weren't ready to oppose it. So Johnson introduced Bob Monroe as his number two man and Raj and me as the guys who would be coming around to collect money.

"Any questions?" he asked when he was done.

"Yeah," said a man in the back. He was a dark-skinned Latino wearing a white muscle T-shirt. "Who the fuck d'you think you are?"

Johnson smiled calmly. "You know who we are, Rafael. We're the guys who can make life good for you."

"Life's already good." He looked around the room for support. Three or four of the others nodded but no one said anything.

Johnson kept the smile. "Any other questions?"

"So, what happens?" said a guy in a sweatshirt and tattoos that reached from his collar to his chin. "Once a week you come to the neighborhood and we line up with our dollar bills?"

Johnson answered like he was talking to a smart student. "Each week you collect the money yourselves, based on the list of names you've given us. Then Raj and Joe come out and meet with a representative from your gang and collect it. The representative could be you or it could be someone else. There will be extra benefits for the representative."

"Like what?" called someone else.

"Like extra protection from us and a little money back directly to you."

Rafael, the big Latino man, said, "We don't need protection."

Again, Johnson smiled, though you could see that his patience was running out. "Then you just get the satisfaction of playing by the rules."

A skinny man in jeans and a turtleneck sweater leaned back in his folding chair and looked at me. "I seen you on TV. You the cop killer."

I shook my head. "Must've been someone else."

"No, no," he said cheerfully. "It was you. They said you also shot another cop. Didn't kill him, though."

It would do no good to explain that I hadn't shot Bill Gubman, that I'd seen someone else shoot him and, depending on who you talked to, I either was responsible for allowing him to get shot or was the one who saved his life. I said, "Now would be a good time to shut up."

He grinned. "Yeah, you the guy on TV."

Monroe smiled. "It's true that Joe killed a man last week and that the man was a cop," he said, "but he hasn't been charged and he won't be." I'd played my part though I hadn't meant to. Monroe must've figured that a man who could shoot a cop and get away with it would worry even the toughest gang member. That's why I was there.

Rafael, the Latino in the muscle shirt, wasn't worried, though. He shook his head. "I'm not giving you no money."

Johnson shook his head too. "Yes, I think you are."

"Yeah? When's that?"

A happy idea occurred to Johnson. "What the hell. Tonight.

Before you leave, each of you will pay your first ten dollars. You'll see how easy it is."

The other gang members mumbled and looked at each other. Three of them fished into their pockets and pulled out a bill or two. Rafael watched them, disgusted. Then he shrugged, stood up, and made to reach into his pocket for his wallet.

He didn't complete the action.

He spun, picked up the chair he'd been sitting on, and threw it through a plate-glass window facing the back deck.

In a flash, Johnson, Monroe, and Raj pulled out guns that they'd hidden under tables and chairs. If you'd blinked you would've thought they were magic. They pointed the guns at Rafael.

Rafael's partner and three other men in the crowd pulled out guns and pointed them at Johnson, Monroe, and Raj. Not as fast but just as deadly.

I fished in the front of my pants but couldn't get at the Ruger fast enough to make a difference.

The men with the guns faced off, no one moving, no one saying a word.

Then the door from the back deck opened.

Johnson, Monroe, Raj, and the gang members swung so their guns pointed at the two men and the woman who walked through it.

The men were Peter Finley and the other cop who'd been checking for weapons when we came in. They held the woman by the wrists and ignored the guns that were pointing at them. "We found her outside," Finley said to Johnson. Then to everyone else, "Anyone know who she is?"

I raised my hand slowly.

"Hi, Joe," the woman said.

"Hi, Lucinda."

Johnson kept cool. He lowered his gun before anyone else and set it on the table in front of him, harmless for the moment but still in easy reach. Three of the gang members lowered their guns. Monroe and Raj tucked theirs away. Rafael's partner pointed his at Johnson until the room calmed, then tipped it toward the floor but with his finger still on the trigger.

Johnson cocked his head and looked at Lucinda. "What are you doing here?"

She said nothing.

"I asked her to come," I lied.

Johnson glared at me and turned to the crowd. "If we'd all do as we're told, this would work a lot better." He looked from face to face to see if everyone was listening, and added, "That's my nice way of warning you not to ignore me." Again, he looked at me. "We'll talk about this later." Then, back to the crowd, "There's a bed in the back. Which one of you wants her?"

Uneasy laughter filled the room. A few of the gang members volunteered. Two offered to share her. Lucinda pulled against the hands that were holding her wrists. The skinny man who'd said he saw me on TV spoke to Johnson, "That ain't funny and it ain't cool."

Johnson smiled at him and turned to Finley. "Would you please walk the lady to her car?"

"I'll take her," I said.

He turned on me. "No," he said. "You stay here."

Lucinda gave me a look and a nod to say it was all right.

I figured she had a better chance if she went with Finley alone than if I crossed Johnson. I said, "Whatever."

Finley and Lucinda left and Johnson turned back to Rafael. His voice was calm but vicious. "You fucked up big. We invite you to talk and you start throwing furniture. Look around and start thinking. All these other guys are in. For a few bucks each they're buying security and peace of mind. They're eliminating the competition. They can do their business and we'll leave them alone. You know what we'll do with all that time we save when we're not hassling them? We'll be busting *you*. Six months from now, there won't be anything left of you and your friends."

If Johnson's speech worried Rafael, he didn't show it. He gestured to his partner and the two headed for the same door Lucinda and Finley had just used. As Rafael stepped outside, he flipped his middle finger at Johnson.

Johnson laughed and said, "Hey, Rafael."

Rafael and his partner turned.

Johnson grabbed his gun from the table and fired it. The partner's head snapped back, struck by a piece of metal that weighed about ten grams but hit harder than a truck.

Rafael opened his mouth to scream but no sound came out. He looked down at his companion. Everyone else looked too. The man's face was half gone. Bone, brain, and blood spilled from the broken shell that had been his skull. The skinny man who knew me from TV said, "Fuuuck!" The others said nothing but looked like they agreed with him.

Then Rafael ran. No one from Johnson's crew stopped him or went after him.

Johnson lowered his gun, stared at me, and spoke to the crowd. "In case anyone's wondering, that's an example of what happens if you break the rules." Then he asked, "Does anyone else want to drop out now?"

No one moved.

"Okay," he said. "Ten bucks apiece tonight. Next week, Joe and Raj will want a list of active members and ten dollars for each of them. Same thing the following week and every week after it. With a little organization, life will be easy for you guys."

"For you too," someone called out.

"Yes," Johnson said. "For us, too."

We sat in the living room after the gang members left, their spinning tires spitting gravel from the driveway, their stereos blasting music. Finley had come back in and nailed a piece of plywood over the broken window. We'd picked up the empty beer cans. We'd mopped the floor and deck where Rafael's partner fell. Three men had gone to the garage and returned with shovels. They'd carried the body of the partner to the beach and, in less than a half hour, had covered him with sand in a hole five feet deep. Deep enough to keep the smell down and the wild animals out. Deep enough to keep the winter storms from exposing the remains.

Now, Johnson and Monroe seemed thoughtful but Raj and Finley laughed easily and looked happy, like they'd escaped a bloody battle without getting wounded. So did the other guys in Johnson's crew.

The duct tape had come loose on my thigh, so I ripped away the rest of it and took out the Ruger.

Johnson turned on me and said, "What the fuck were you thinking?"

The question sounded rhetorical so I didn't answer.

He gestured at Finley but kept his eyes on me. "Peter could have shot your friend just as easily as bringing her in for you to identify. Then you would've had a dead friend and we would've had another mess to clean up—smaller than the one you made at Southshore but big enough. You're making it hard for us to work with you."

Again I said nothing. I figured that cleaning up another body when he'd just splattered one across Finley's living room and deck wouldn't be a lot of extra work, but telling him that seemed like a bad idea. And explaining that I'd told Lucinda not to follow me—that she must have hung back when the FBI van followed us when we shot across Congress Parkway, fallen in behind us when we'd reappeared, and come on her own—would just make him ask why I'd told her about my evening plans to begin with.

"And who told you to bring a gun?" he said.

I said, "I figured the idea for this meeting was just crazy enough that someone like Rafael would throw a chair through a window. I wanted to be ready."

Johnson sighed. "You got the first part right, but we expected that. We were ready for it. Were you? Next time don't disobey orders. Or if you do, do it right. If you're going to carry a gun, make sure you can get to it. If it weren't for me, Monroe, and Raj, you would've had ten holes in your body before you finished jerking off and got the gun out of your pants."

"I could've gotten it out," I said.

"You could've shot yourself in the balls." He turned to Monroe. "You brought this guy in. He's your responsibility."

Monroe glared at him.

"No more fuckups," Johnson said.

Raj interrupted. "You think we've got a problem with Rafael?"

Johnson shook his head. "He's easy. We know where he stands. It's the ones who stayed quiet that we've got to worry about." He looked back at me. "Them and anyone we don't know well enough to count on."

"Why did you shoot Rafael's partner?" I asked. "Why not Rafael himself?"

Johnson spoke slowly, like he figured I needed special help. "You don't shoot a gang leader unless you want the rest of his gang to be gunning for you. Rafael's partner made the point."

Monroe nodded, then stood and set out the plans for the next three weeks. Raj would get directions from him, and the two of us would start visiting gang representatives. Finley was checking out a building site that looked almost ready for wiring, which meant almost ready for a late-night visit from the crew. At the end of three weeks, we would meet again at The Spa Club to adjust our plans—unless anything went seriously wrong in the meantime. If that happened, we would meet sooner.

When Monroe finished, Finley raised a finger and Johnson nodded to him.

"About three miles west of here, before the highway, there's a construction site. Looks like it'll be a processing plant of some kind. A lot of pipe. Probably a lot of wire. It looks good."

Johnson nodded again. "When?"

"Tonight?"

"Without checking out the place first?"

"There are no guards," Finley said. "We go in and out. Snatch and grab. Leave behind anything we can't take in five minutes."

Johnson thought about it, then shrugged. "Why not?"

I said, "You're planning on bringing in thousands of dollars a day from the gangs. Why bother with this stuff?"

Johnson looked at Monroe like he couldn't believe Monroe

had brought me into the group. Then he said, like I'd missed the obvious, "This is the fun part."

The others laughed.

Raj grinned and slapped my shoulder. "Come on. It's play-time."

SIXTEEN

WE DROVE IN FIVE SUVs and vans back through Pleasant Prairie, past bare farm fields, and through the industrial strip. We turned onto a dark road with a street sign that said COUNTY HIGHWAY H, drove past a bunch of single-story white-sided factories and more farm fields, then swung to the shoulder by a construction lot surrounded by a tall chain-link fence. The top of the fence was lined with barbed wire.

Lights strung around the lot showed a main building that matched the ones we'd passed—single story and white—but it had three smokestacks at one end and a tall structure next to it, connected to the main building by a series of wide pipes. A temporary aluminum storage shed stood where I figured a parking lot would be. Next to it were piles of pipe and sheet metal.

Raj pulled to the front of the line of cars but stopped short of a pole that held a video camera focused on a gated driveway onto the lot.

He reached under the driver's seat, pulled out a pair of

work gloves, and slipped them on. "There's another pair under your seat," he said.

He got out, took a piece of steel pipe from the back of the SUV, and walked behind the pole that held the video camera. He smashed the camera. Pieces of metal and plastic flew to the ground and when the camera stopped turning it faced toward the clouds. Raj came back and exchanged the pipe for a pair of bolt cutters, went to the gate, and clipped the chain, then swung the gate open.

He ran back to the SUV and we led the others onto the lot.

We poured out of the vehicles and spread across the lot, scavenging for copper and anything else valuable that wasn't bolted down. "All right," yelled Johnson. "We've got five minutes."

Finley shouted for assistance. Under a plastic tarp outside the storage shed, he'd found a small store of copper piping. In two trips, we loaded it into the back of one of the vans.

"Four minutes!" Johnson shouted.

The wind had picked up and the night had gotten cold, but we took off our coats and tossed them into our vehicles. We stripped the lot of everything that could be carried by hand and fit so the van and SUV doors would shut.

Raj went to the SUV and came back to the aluminum shed with a crowbar. He rammed the end into the gap between the door and the frame and threw his shoulder against the bar. The door didn't move.

"Help me!" he said.

I stood on the other side of the crowbar and pulled as he pushed.

The door slowly pulled away from the frame until the lock bolts cleared their housings. The door swung free.

Raj dropped the crowbar and grinned. "Thanks." He reached inside the door and flipped on a light.

"Three minutes!" Johnson shouted.

The contractors had partly finished the inside of the shed. At the back end, they'd built three small rooms complete with locked doors. The shed smelled like new lumber and a chemical I didn't recognize. A stack of insulated cable stood near the door. A large pile of two-by-fours stood against a side wall. Other stacks of sealed cardboard boxes stood in the middle of the large room.

I went for the insulated cable.

"Leave that," Raj said. "Get those." He pointed at a pile of gray metal boxes.

"What are they?"

"Transformers. Worth a couple hundred apiece."

We carried a dozen of them to the SUV.

When we finished, Raj brought the crowbar inside. He went to one of the locked doors. A sign that hung on it said WARNING— GUARD DOGS. He jammed the end of the crowbar between the door and the frame.

"What are you doing?" I said.

He cocked his head toward the door. "Listen," he said. "No dogs."

"So?"

"So, someone's using the sign to keep people away from this room. That means something valuable's inside. Could be electronics. Could be cash." He pushed the crowbar deeper.

"Two minutes!" Johnson shouted but a moment later he yelled, "Forget it! Let's go!"

"What's wrong?" I said.

Raj shrugged. "A car's coming or there's something on the police frequency."

"Come on!" yelled Johnson outside. "Go, go, go!"

Raj laid his weight against the crowbar.

"Come on," I said.

"In a moment." The door started to separate from the frame.

Outside, the other men were shouting.

Raj eased the crowbar, reached into his pocket, and tossed me a ring of keys. "Start the car." He went back to work on the door.

I ran to the shed exit and looked back at Raj as he pried the door and it ripped out from the frame. Raj stood for a moment like he expected gold coins to pour over him.

Then three German shepherds lunged out.

"Fuck!" Raj yelled and one of the dogs landed on his chest. Raj fell back and rolled across the floor, the dog on top of him.

I started toward him but another dog came after me. I sprinted out the door to the SUV. As I fired up the engine, I looked toward the county highway. Two sets of headlights were approaching.

The other SUVs and vans spun their tires on the dirt, snaked across the lot, and shot through the gate and onto the road, heading away from the headlights. I followed them, but when I reached the gate, I hit the brakes. Two dogs, maybe three were ripping into Raj inside the storage shed.

I shifted into reverse, bounced back over the dirt, and looked over my shoulder in time to see Raj run from the shed, blood on his face, the dogs behind him, lunging at his hands and legs like he was a wild animal that they meant to bring down. I headed toward him but it seemed like he couldn't see the SUV.

He ran for the fence and, when he reached it, climbed and kept climbing until his clothes hung up in the barbed wire stretched across the top. The dogs stood against the fence on their hind legs and barked and howled.

With the crowbar I might be able to clear them. But the crowbar was lying on the floor inside the shed.

I drove the SUV to the fence, shined the headlights on the dogs. Raj hung onto the top of the fence, bleeding, his face wild with fear. The dogs ignored me.

The headlights on the road were a couple of blocks away.

I pulled the SUV away from the fence, turned it around, and shifted into reverse. I backed toward the fence until two of the dogs ran to the side and the other yelped and then followed them. The rear end of the SUV touched the fence and I opened my window and yelled, "Climb onto the roof."

After a few seconds, Raj yelled, "Can't."

I leaned out the window. Raj's clothes were tangled in the barbed wire. The German shepherds were running back and forth, whining, looking for a way to get to him. The cars on the road slowed as they reached the open gate. One of them pulled onto the driveway so its headlights shined on the scene.

I tried opening the driver-side door but a German shepherd came at me. I slammed the door, then squeezed myself through the driver-side window and pulled myself onto the roof. Raj was watching the dogs like they might climb the fence and eat him there. I crawled toward him. "Give me your hand," I said and he reached toward me, his eyes still on the dogs. I cleared his sleeve from the barbs, cleared one of his pant legs.

"Get me down," he said.

A voice yelled from the open window of the car that had

pulled onto the lot. A woman's voice. "I've called for help," the woman said.

Help of the kind she would have called was the last thing we needed. "Thanks!" I yelled back.

I helped Raj free his other leg and then his arm, and he inched onto the roof of the SUV. "Can you slide into the window?" I asked.

He shook his head.

"Then hold tight."

I slid into the window and drove away from the fence. As we passed the car that had pulled onto the construction lot, a woman in her sixties watched the SUV with the bloodied man on top as though it was a strange, horrible animal that had gotten loose in southern Wisconsin. I waved to her. Her window went up.

A man about the same age sat in the car outside the gate, speaking into a cell phone. Probably to the cops.

A quarter mile later, I pulled to the shoulder. Raj crawled across the roof, slid down the windshield onto the hood, climbed down, and tried his feet on the ground. They held him.

"Jesus!" he whispered more to himself than to me. "I should be dead."

The SUV headlights showed blood on his face and right leg, deep scratches on his arms, but, unless he had worse cuts under his clothes, nothing that would make him bleed to death, maybe nothing that even needed stitches.

"Are you all right?" I asked anyway.

He looked at me long, like it took an effort for him to remember who I was. Then he nodded and said again, "I should be dead."

He stepped away from the SUV toward a ditch that separated the road from a farm field. He looked up at the clouded sky. If the woman and the man at the construction lot had given the 911 operator the kind of information I figured they'd given, two or three police cars were headed our way. Probably an ambulance and a fire truck too.

"Get in the car," I said.

"I should be dead," Raj said and got into the passenger seat.

I got in too and punched the accelerator.

The dark stubble fields gave way to the factories with empty, brightly lighted parking lots. As I turned from the county highway toward the road back to Chicago, red emergency lights flashed in the distance. I hit the accelerator again and kept it down until we reached the on-ramp.

We drove south for awhile without talking. When I glanced at Raj, he was staring out the window at the sky, like he did at the side of the highway. I wondered what he was looking at, what he saw, but I didn't ask.

A couple of minutes after we crossed the Illinois state line, he said, "That was the stupidest thing I've ever done."

"Yeah? Which part of it?"

For awhile he said nothing. Then, "I hate dogs. Ever since I was a kid."

"Who would've known they were there?" I said. "They didn't bark."

"They didn't fucking breathe! But the sign—I could've believed the sign."

"Do you need a doctor?"

He felt his face and head with his fingers, looking at the blood that came away on his hands, then felt the rest of his body, arms, and legs. "No," he said. "I'm good."

Good was an exaggeration. "You want me to stop at a gas station? You can clean up."

He shook his head. "I'll do it when we get back."

For the next half hour we were quiet again. The headlights shined on the gray asphalt, and, except for the occasional lighted signs in front of roadside businesses, we drove through a tunnel of darkness. The car smelled like the salt of blood and sweat and the sweet plastic of the new electronics we'd stolen.

When the orange glow of Chicago sharpened in front of us, I felt the tension of the night ease. I looked at Raj again. He was staring at the road now. He felt my eyes on him and he turned and his bloodied lips gave me a half smile.

"Thanks," he said.

"No problem," I said.

"You saved me."

I shrugged. "What was I going to do? Leave you there?"

He shrugged too. "Thanks anyway." What neither of us said was that his friends in Johnson's crew *had* left him there.

SEVENTEEN

AS WE DROVE INTO the city, Raj's cell phone rang. The dashboard clock said the time was 2:11 A.M. From his end of the conversation, I figured he was talking to Johnson. Johnson was telling him what to do and when to do it.

Raj listened to it all, never telling him what had happened after the rest of them left. Then he said, "I need a half hour, maybe forty minutes." His voice was calm but I heard an edge of anger in it.

Johnson must not have liked what he heard.

"Because that's what I need," Raj insisted.

Johnson apparently backed down.

"All right," Raj added and hung up. He shook his head, disgusted.

"What now?" I asked.

He told me to get off the highway on the Northside, then directed me through the dark streets to a little house on Oakley Avenue. I pulled to the curb.

"Come inside," he said.

The place was a beige single story with an air-conditioning unit in a dormer window in front and a half dozen concrete steps to the front porch. A light fixture, mounted next to the door, shined on the sidewalk. Another light was on behind the shades in the front room.

"Your house?" I asked as he unlocked the door.

He nodded.

The inside was comfortable, but no more than. The fabric on the living room sofa showed wear. So did the fabric on the easy chair. A coffee table had stacks of magazines on top and needed dusting. A plastic bin of Legos stood next to the sofa. A carpeted stairway led to an attic room. Nothing in the place said a dishonest cop was living there.

Raj went into an adjoining kitchen, came back with two cans of beer, and handed me one. He popped the tab and raised the can in a toast. I raised mine too. "To dogs," I said.

He almost laughed. "Not unless they're stuffed and mounted."

A bedroom door that connected to the living room opened, and a woman stepped in. She looked no older than twenty-five and wore a little blue nightgown. She had a tattoo of a snake on her upper thigh. Another, of a star, dipped into the nightgown from her breast. She had blond hair and full lips, and her eyes said she hadn't been sleeping.

"Where the hell—" she started, then saw the blood on Raj and noticed me. She stopped and her anger melted. "What—" she tried again, but that was all that came out.

Raj went to her. "Ellen, this is Joe. Joe, this is Ellen."

"Glad to meet you," she said. Her eyes stayed on her husband. She didn't sound glad to meet me.

She reached to Raj's face and touched where the dog had bitten him.

He flinched, took her hand, and removed it from him. "I'm okay," he said. "I just need to clean up."

He went into the bedroom she'd come out of. She turned and gave me a long look like she was sure I'd injured Raj myself, then followed him in.

For awhile, the house was quiet except for the murmur of voices from the bedroom. I looked at the pictures on the wall: framed photos of an olive-skinned woman I figured was Raj's mother, another woman who could have been a sister, a guy who definitely was a brother, a young kid who either was Raj's son or a nephew. I looked at a glass-fronted china cabinet. The plates and coffee cups were cheap, but you display what you've got.

The voices in the bedroom got louder.

Raj's wife said, "He killed a cop."

"He's—"

The voices fell to angry whispers.

A boy about seven years old wandered down the stairs from the attic bedroom. He wore red pajama pants that looked like long underwear and a matching shirt. He had sleep in his eyes. He gave me a shy smile and disappeared back up the stairs.

A minute later, he came back down a couple steps.

"Hi," I said.

"Hi," he said.

"It's late. You should be in bed."

"Where's my dad?" he asked.

I nodded toward the bedroom. "In there."

He came down the stairs, stopped on the bottom step, looked at me like I was a danger he didn't want to face on his way across the room. I stepped away to clear the path. "What's your name?" I said.

He eyed me. "Farid." Then he darted across the room.

"Like your dad."

He nodded and knocked on the door.

"I have a boy named Jason," I tried, but he just stared at the door.

His mother opened it and, when she saw him, scooped him into her arms and whisked him upstairs like I was a disease she needed to protect him from.

As they disappeared, Raj wandered in. He'd cleaned himself and slicked his hair down with water. He limped a little and his pant leg bulged over his left ankle where he'd wrapped it with gauze. He'd taped a butterfly bandage over the skin above his lips. He had a Band-Aid on his left hand. Other than that, his sleeves and jeans covered his wounds.

He tried a smile. "You ready?"

FOR FIVE MILES NORTHWEST out of the Loop, brick warehouses line both sides of the Chicago River. They were built at a time when men on the docks unloaded cargo that had come in through the locks from Lake Michigan or loaded it for the reverse trip. Here and there in the past couple of years, a condo development or a restaurant had shouldered in with promises of a water view, but mostly the brick buildings stood empty or half used. On a cold November night, even the bums who'd found a spot on the floor in the buildings during the spring, summer, and fall had cleared out for shelters with central heating.

Raj and I drove to a warehouse built on a spot where the river swings to the west. The lights were off outside the building. Leaves and garbage had clumped on the parking lot like no one had parked or driven there in years.

"The quicker we get rid of this stuff, the less chance we have of getting caught," Raj said.

I backed the SUV to an aluminum garage door and Raj got out, pushed a button on an intercom, and spoke into it. The garage door rattled up, metal clashing against metal.

Johnson's crew stood inside with three tall black men, one in a pin-striped suit and tie, the others in zippered nylon warm-up suits. One of them yelled at me to back the car between the SUVs and vans already in the warehouse. Before I cleared the threshold, the aluminum garage door started down.

Ceiling lamps high in the steel rafters lighted the front end of the building. The back end disappeared in shadows. Steel shelves made neat aisles, rising from the concrete floor high toward the ceiling. Wooden pallets on the shelves held electronics, tools, and building supplies.

One of the guys in warm-up suits opened the back of the SUV and brought a transformer that we'd stolen to the man in pinstripes. The man looked it over and offered Johnson ninety dollars. Johnson said a hundred fifty. They agreed on a hundred ten. The guys in warm-ups unloaded the rest of the transformers onto a pallet set on a forklift.

Raj and I joined the other men. Monroe looked Raj over. "What the hell happened to you?" he asked.

"Nothing," Raj said.

A grin spread across Monroe's face. "Come on, let's see the battle wounds."

Raj shrugged and hoisted his pant leg, exposing his ankle. Blood had soaked through the gauze.

Finley gave a low whistle.

"What else?" said Monroe.

Raj lied. "That's it."

Finley stepped toward him, grinning too, and reached toward his cheek. "Such a pretty face too—"

Raj grabbed Finley's wrist.

The grin fell from Finley's face. For a few seconds, it seemed that they would fight.

Then Finley said, "All right." He shook his wrist free.

Monroe turned to the other men. "Who's hungry?" he said. "I'm buying breakfast."

THE GOLDEN NUGGET FAMILY Restaurant on North Clark Street is in a dirty brown brick building with a faded yellow sign. At four in the morning, the clientele includes hookers done with their final customers, insomniac transvestites, and men living on the street who can't take any more of the night and the cold so they scrape together enough quarters and dimes to buy a cup of coffee and an egg. But day or night, the Golden Nugget serves the best pancakes on the Northside.

We pulled four tables together in a back room usually reserved for birthday parties. The waitresses knew Johnson's crew well enough to joke with them and exchange hugs. They also knew them well enough to leave us alone once we'd ordered.

We'd tossed our jackets over empty chairs. A couple of guys had kicked their feet up on the vinyl seat cushions. Finley rested his chin on his hands, yawned, and closed his eyes. We could've been a group of undercover cops relaxing at the end of a tough shift. Except Johnson had a stack of cash in front of him and he was dividing it into smaller stacks, one for each of us.

"How much did we make?" Monroe asked.

Johnson kept dealing bills into piles. "Eighteen thousand, four hundred."

Finley opened his eyes. "For four and a half minutes of work. What's that per hour?"

Monroe said to Johnson, "You could've gotten more for the transformers."

Johnson looked annoyed. "What are you saying?"

"I'm saying we're not in business to make the buyer happy."

"If the buyer is unhappy, we're out of business."

Monroe mumbled, "Plus you wouldn't pick up a little extra on the side."

Johnson snapped. "Don't ever fucking say that!"

"Okay, maybe not. I'm just saying—"

"Never," Johnson said, standing up at the table, leaning over Monroe. "Don't say it unless you're ready to prove it, not if you want to work with me."

Monroe didn't look worried. "I'm just saying we've got only one buyer and you brought him in. He gets the price he wants to pay, more or less. I'd like to have more than one buyer. We'd make more money."

Johnson shook his head like he couldn't believe Monroe's stupidity. "Do you know another buyer?"

Monroe admitted he didn't.

"Until you do, shut the fuck up, okay?" Johnson sat down and continued dealing out the bills.

A minute or two after we'd stuffed our stacks of bills into

our pockets, the waitresses came in with trays of steaming pancakes, eggs, bacon, and toast. A large-breasted gray-haired waitress in her late fifties leaned over me and filled my cup with coffee, as hot as the night was cold. For a moment I lost my appetite. Then I tore into my food like I'd spent my night burning energy with gang members, vicious dogs, and thieves.

EIGHTEEN

I CLIMBED THE STEPS to the back porch of my house as the first sunlight brightened the sky. My legs ached. The rest of me too. The night had drained the last of me and I wondered if I should climb into bed or just go inside and lie down on the kitchen floor. Twelve hours of sleep would help. Fourteen wouldn't hurt.

I unlocked the door, let myself in.

I stopped. "Damn," I said.

The three FBI agents who'd stopped Lucinda and me as we'd left Daley Plaza were sitting at the kitchen table. They had cups of steaming coffee in front of them.

"Good morning!" said the lead agent, cheerful, like he'd gotten a good night's sleep.

"'Morning," I said and went to the table and sat with them.

The agent tapped his coffee cup. "We helped ourselves. Hope you don't mind."

"Hey, my house is your house," I said.

"That's how we like to look at it."

"What else did you help yourselves to?"

"Nothing yet. We just arrived." He sipped from his cup. "It would be nice to say that we were surprised that you weren't here, but that would be a lie."

The kitchen was warm. I wondered what the agents would do if I laid my head on the table and went to sleep. "You did a lousy job of following me last night."

The lead agent lifted his eyebrows just enough to tell me I was an idiot. "Didn't matter. We knew where you went. You know, transporting stolen goods over state lines is a federal crime. It's good for a couple years in jail."

"How about breaking into a man's house and helping your-self to coffee? That's got to be worth a couple of months."

One of the other agents, the heavyset guy who Lucinda had decked, picked up his cup. He glared at me. Then he flung the cup at the kitchen sink. It smashed against the tile backsplash.

That woke me up. "Vandalism," I said. "A couple more months."

He pushed his chair back and stood like he was coming after me, but the lead agent put a hand on his arm and he sat down. "We can take you in now for crossing the state line, or we can let it slide. Up to you."

He'd mentioned nothing about the meeting with the gang representatives. I wondered if he knew about it too. I shrugged and stood. "It was a long night. I'm going to bed."

He stayed in his chair. "We want you to work with us."

"Like you said yesterday."

"We say it again today. Plus we say we'll pay you."

"And?"

"What else do you want?" he said.

"Protection. Total immunity." Bill Gubman said he wanted to keep the Feds out of the investigation. But when the Feds showed up in my kitchen at dawn and helped themselves to my coffee, I needed to calculate the risks of staying quiet.

"We can protect you—at least some. We can't promise immunity."

"You can promise me anything you want."

"Not that."

"You should talk to my lawyer. His name's Larry Weiss. I'll give you his number."

"Fuck your lawyer."

"Fuck my lawyer?"

He nodded.

"Well, then, fuck you." I turned to go to bed.

Three chairs scraped against the floor. I spun, thinking they were coming for me. They weren't. They went to the kitchen drawers, pulled them out, and dumped them on the floor.

"Now that's foolish," I said.

They shuffled the silverware and dishtowels with their feet like they were looking for something. Then they opened the cabinets and cleared the pots and mixing bowls. The lead agent went to the pantry and swept the food off the shelves.

"What are you looking for?" I said.

"A reason to arrest you on charges that will get you more than a couple years."

"We'll find something sooner or later," said the agent who'd smashed my coffee cup.

"Or if we don't," said the third, "we'll bring something in from our van."

"Do you have a search warrant?" I said.

The lead agent stopped knocking things onto the floor and looked me in the eyes. "Now who's being foolish?"

I watched them wreck the kitchen for awhile. Then they went into the hall and headed for Jason's bedroom.

I followed them down the hall. "You don't screw around with a kid's stuff. You go in there and I'll kill you."

They came back up the hall and the lead agent looked at me long and hard. I looked at him the same. Then his face softened. "Okay," he said.

I breathed out, relieved.

The other agents brushed past me, heading back toward the kitchen.

Then, one of them turned, grabbed my arms from behind, and shoved me against the hallway wall. The other drew his gun and held it against my head.

The lead agent went into Jason's room. Drawers fell from the dresser. Toys knocked to the floor. Books tumbled from the shelves. He spent ten minutes destroying the space Jason had made for himself with me, away from his mom and everything he'd known for eleven years.

My muscles tightened. A 9mm pistol pressed against the back of my head. My back and the insides of my legs sweated. I said nothing.

When the lead agent finished with the room, he came into the hall and got close to my ear. "You were right," he said, soft. "That was a waste of time."

I spun. My fist caught him in his face and blood burst from his nose. The 9mm slipped from the back of my head. The agent who'd held it regripped it and pointed it at my chest, a look of panic on his face.

Fury rose in the lead agent's face. "You fucking idiot." He turned and went down the hall to the bathroom.

I slumped against the wall. "First time you've done this?" I said to the man with the gun.

He said nothing.

"You can relax now," I said.

He said, "One call to DCFS, and we can take the kid away from you."

Water ran in the bathroom sink and a minute later the lead agent returned with a bloody towel pressed against his face.

"There's your charge," said the agent who'd smashed the cup. "Assaulting a federal officer."

The lead agent ignored him. "Let's go back to the kitchen," he said to me.

We kicked the food and pots out of the way and sat at the table.

"You like working with Earl Johnson?" he asked.

I shrugged. "Beats some of the company I've been spending time with."

"Do you know who he is?"

I'd known Johnson since we went to the academy together. "What do you mean?"

He mopped his bloody nose with my bathroom towel. "He might be involved in more than you think he is."

I considered that. Maybe Johnson really was running a side operation of the kind that Bill Gubman was fabricating. Maybe he was pulling a double scam, one against the police department and one against the rest of his crew. Maybe Bill's plans to set him up were unnecessary because Johnson was already guilty. He wouldn't be the first thief who dipped his fingers into his friends' pockets.

I smiled.

"What's funny?"

"Nothing," I said. "Tell me about him."

"The day that you shot our informant at Southshore Village, he reported that he'd found out something important about Johnson. We wanted to ask him about that when we met with him after the robbery. Thanks to you, we never got to meet. Do you know what he found out?"

I shook my head. "I'd never met your guy when I shot him."

He nodded. "And you've seen nothing interesting about Johnson since then?"

I had suspicions about Johnson, no more. "I've seen a lot that's interesting. But no."

"Would you tell me if you did?"

I thought about that. "I don't know."

He stood and pulled a card out of his wallet, said, "Call when you're ready to talk—or if you need help."

I looked at the card. It had two phone numbers, one for his field office and one for his cell. It said FBI in bold letters. It also gave his name—Stuart Felicano.

"Is that your real name?" I asked.

He shrugged. "Sure."

I gestured at his two partners. "How about these guys?"

"Just telephone me." He pressed my bathroom towel against his bleeding nose. "Can I borrow this?"

I shrugged. "My house is your house."

They let themselves out through the back door.

I sat for a few minutes at the kitchen table and considered what to do.

I should call Bill Gubman and tell him about the FBI. I should call Larry Weiss and ask for his legal opinion about how to avoid screwing myself more than I'd already done. I should call Lucinda and see how she'd spent her evening after Peter Finley escorted her to her car in Wisconsin. I should call Corrine and tell her I loved her. I should call to check on Jason at the hospital. I should sweep the mess from the kitchen floor and put the pots and pans where they belonged. I should pick up Jason's room so he would never know an FBI agent ransacked it. I should pack a suitcase and drive south until the air warmed and my memory dulled.

I stood and went to my bedroom, climbed into bed, and closed my eyes.

NINETEEN

THE SUN WAS HIGH and my room was bright. The clock said 11:38. I'd slept for four hours. If I'd dreamed anything, my exhaustion had swallowed it. But when I opened my eyes, I ripped awake like out of a nightmare.

I got up and showered, cleaned the mess in the kitchen, and scrambled three eggs, my second breakfast of the day. Then I straightened Jason's room. Stuart Felicano had done less of a job on it than he might have. Nothing was broken, nothing hard to clean. He probably hadn't expected to turn up anything. He'd meant to pressure me. His card sat on the kitchen table. I wondered what would make me call the numbers on it.

I drove downtown to my office and rode the elevator to the eighth floor. The owner of the secretarial school stood at her office door with a student.

"Hi, Roselle," I said.

She ushered the student inside and closed the door. Before the TV news and the papers had started calling me a cop killer, she'd sometimes flirted with me and once had invited me in to talk with her and allowed me out only when I told her I was still involved with my ex-wife.

In my office, the red light on the answering machine was flashing, and a small brown box and a stack of mail stood on the floor where the building super left them. My bottle of Jim Beam Black and the Baggie of cocaine waited for me in a file cabinet drawer. I ignored it all. I went to my window. The early afternoon sun shined warm on the insurance building across the street. In the distance, through a gap between buildings, Lake Michigan gleamed flat and bright as a golden mirror. From eight stories up, the city looked like a place where you could live a reasonable life.

I picked up the package and stack of mail and put them on my desk, then punched the button on the answering machine. A digitized voice told me I had eight messages. Two of them were hate calls, telling me what the callers thought guys who shot cops should do to themselves, including things that even a contortionist couldn't accomplish. Three messages were reporters seeking comments. One message was a crank who said he was glad I'd shot David Russo and if I wanted an assistant he was available. One message was from a woman who wanted to hire me to find her runaway son. I figured she must not read newspapers or watch the news. I wrote down her number in case I survived Earl Johnson and the FBI. The last message was from Bill Gubman, who'd called ten minutes before I arrived at my office. He said he'd tried me at home and I didn't answer, and if I got his message I should call right away—it was important. It must be, I figured, since he was willing to risk calling me when I was setting up Johnson. So I called the 1st District Station. The man who picked up the phone said Bill wasn't available but he'd relay a message if I wanted to leave one. I told him where Bill could reach me and hung up.

Then I called Corrine at her landscape business. No answer. So I called her cell phone. She said she was heading into a meeting with a client who owned a Lincoln Park town house with a backyard garden bigger than a tennis court, though you would never guess it from the street. The client wanted Corrine to winterize the beds and prepare them to grow prize-winning roses in the spring. While life died around me, Corrine made things grow.

"That sounds like a good job," I said.

"The client's wasting her money," she said. "The garden will never get enough sun for roses. Hey, she's coming. Can we talk later?"

"Anytime," I said and we hung up.

Next I dialed Children's Memorial and asked for Jason's room. The operator put me through to a nurse in his ward, who told me that they no longer had a patient by Jason's name. A moment of fear pulsed through me before she added that his doctor had released him in the morning. I called Mom's house and she said Jason was sleeping and why didn't I join them for dinner at seven. I said I would be there.

Lucinda picked up her cell phone on the third ring. "You told me you'd call when you got back last night," she said.

"And you told me you weren't going to follow me last night."

"I followed you because I care about you. You *didn't* call me because you *don't* care about me."

A nice try. "I told you not to follow me because I care about you. I didn't call because three FBI agents were sitting in my kitchen when I got home and when they left I passed out for a few hours. So in a way I'm just getting back from last night now and this is your call."

I'd exaggerated the circumstances but she said, "Oh."

I filled in some of the details about the hours since Peter Finley walked her from the gang meeting to her car, then asked what she'd been doing.

"For starters," she said, "Finley asked me out on a date."

"You're kidding."

She pretended to be stung. "Why would I be? He said any woman who could tail Raj for sixty miles without being seen was someone he wanted to know. He asked me out for dinner."

"How did you tail us, by the way?"

"When you were downtown, you had your turn signal on at Congress Parkway. Then you spotted the FBI van and went straight. I figured you'd be coming back to Congress. So I waited and followed you when you reappeared."

"You *are* smart enough to date."

"I know."

"You also know that Finley is married with three kids?"

"He said."

"So what did you tell him?"

"This isn't about romance, Joe. This is about getting in closer so we can find out more about him and Johnson's group."

"I know that. So you said yes?"

"We're having dinner tonight."

"I don't like it."

"You don't like it for a good reason? Or you don't like it because you don't want me doing this kind of thing even though you're still with Corrine?"

"Who said I'm still with Corrine?"

"You didn't answer my question."

"I just don't like it."

"Sorry."

"You do anything else since last night besides playing girl-friend to a gangster?"

"Yeah, I talked to some friends in the department about Bob Monroe and Raj. Monroe's worse than his mixed record shows. The story is that when he was in the gang unit he not only bud-died up with some of the gang members but he took sides. One guy who got busted for midlevel dealing offered to trade infor-mation on Monroe for dropped charges. He seemed credible enough that they sent someone from internal affairs to interview him. The guy supposedly said Monroe had set up two mem-bers of La Raza and was present when they died. The guy didn't have evidence. It would've been his word against Mon-roe's, and he supposedly already had a long record. But the interesting thing is that right after the guy told his story, the department moved Monroe to vice *and* they dropped the traf-ficking charges and let the guy go."

"A little too much *supposedly* in there. You think we could find this guy and talk to him?"

"That's another interesting thing. Two days after he got out of jail, someone shot and killed him. No one's been charged with the shooting."

I thought about that for a moment. "Happens all the time to drug dealers," I said.

"Sure it does," she agreed. "And to some more than others."

"Yeah," I said. "What about Raj?"

"No one had anything bad to say about him. Like we thought,

he's an eagle scout except that he's involved with Johnson. Of the four guys I asked, three said he's the person they would go to if they were in trouble and needed help."

"Yeah, for a thief, part-owner of a whorehouse, and racketeer, he seems okay. You get anything else?"

"That's it. I'm going to make more calls, but then I've got to wash my hair, paint my toenails, and get ready for my date."

"Ha," I said as humorlessly as I could and added, "Be careful tonight."

"I will."

"And call me when you get back."

She laughed at that, said, "What are you going to do?"

"Spend about ten more minutes at my office, then go home and try to get more sleep."

She said, "I'll talk with you later then, right?"

"Right," I said and we hung up.

The mail was bills, a catalogue of office equipment, payment for an employee background check I'd done, and more bills. The package had no return address. I had friends in the business who never opened a package without one. Too many unsatisfied customers—the ones whose suspicions about their wives or husbands you'd been unable to confirm, and the ones whose suspicions you'd confirmed. Too much chance that the package would contain something ugly.

I snapped the packing tape and opened the top.

I would have preferred a bomb.

I lifted out a stack of photographs. They were mostly of a woman and David Russo, the cop I'd shot. The photo on top was a formal portrait of them, him in a tuxedo, her in a yellow dress—probably taken at someone else's wedding. The next showed their own wedding, him in another tuxedo, her in white. The next three photos showed them inside and outside a house which I figured must be their own. Dozens more showed them on vacations, with friends, at a birthday party, with a dog. He looked happy. She looked happy. I looked at every one. She'd sent me a record of the life they'd lived together. She wanted me to see what I'd taken away.

I set down the photos and moved the box from my desk. Something shifted inside it—a tissue bundled into a packet.

I took it out and unwrapped it.

"Jesus!" I said.

It was a man's wedding band. It had to be her husband's. Who else's?

Why would she send it to me? What was I supposed to do with it?

I put it on my desk like someone had accused me of trying to steal it, pushed my chair away, and went back to the window. The lake still gleamed calm and gold. Sun still shined on the insurance building.

I went back to the desk, sat, and picked up the ring. I slipped it over the end of my left ring finger, lowered it to the first knuckle, slid it to the second knuckle.

It fit.

Corrine once had slid a ring like this one onto my finger.

I took off the ring and looked at it for awhile. Then I slid it onto my right ring finger, past the second knuckle until it rested against the thin web of skin that holds the hand together. David Russo's wife had sent the ring so I wouldn't forget. It might've been the most valuable thing that she still had from her husband, and she'd sent it to the man who'd killed him. The least I could do was wear it.

Someone knocked at the office door. I jumped. For a

moment, I had the weird feeling that Russo's wife had come to visit.

I felt the unfamiliar weight of the ring as I went to the door and opened it.

Rafael, the Latino gang member who'd challenged Earl Johnson last night, was standing in the corridor.

TWENTY

RAFAEL LOOKED HARD AT my face. "What's wrong with you?"

I tried to look calm. "Nothing. Come in."

He stepped into the office, carrying a small vinyl bag, and looked around like hidden men might jump him. Maybe checking every room he entered had saved him a time or two. He had a marine haircut, short everywhere but a little shorter on the sides than on top. He had a diamond stud in his right earlobe and another diamond clipped high on his outer ear. He had a raised brown spot on his cheek—a mole or a birthmark, something you could identify his corpse with, sooner or later. Except for the brown spot, he probably was handsome.

He sat in the chair I kept for clients and I went to my desk chair. "What can I do for you?" I said.

He put the vinyl bag on my desk. It clunked when it hit the desktop, metal against metal.

"What's that? A gun?"

"Don't be a dickhead. It's money. First payment."

"You've got coins in there?"

"Some. We kick in what we've got."

"I thought you weren't going to pay."

"I won't pay Johnson. But me and my friends don't want to commit suicide by cop, especially a fucked-up cop like Johnson. This is stay-alive money, right?"

"You know I've got to take it back to Johnson, or else it doesn't do you any good."

"So take it to him. But I don't trust him and I won't deal with him."

"Seems like a good call," I said. "Why do you trust me?"

"I don't. But I could find you. You're on the news and you're in the Yellow Pages. I can do two plus two."

I thought about that and asked something that had started nagging me. "You think two plus two equals four in Johnson's scam?"

A corner of his mouth turned up in a smile. "You mean, do I think he's not all he says he is?"

I nodded.

"Hell, yeah."

"What do you think he's up to?"

He shrugged. "As long as it don't get me killed, I don't give a fuck. Seems like you're the one who's got to worry about that."

He glanced at my hands. I realized I was playing with David Russo's ring on my finger and I stopped. I said, "Why don't you trust Johnson?"

He looked up at my eyes, like he was figuring how much to tell me. He said, "We used to deal with Monroe. Monroe's a fuckhead but we knew what to expect from him, right? Then

Johnson shows up and says he's the man, not Monroe. He says he won't bother us if we pay him, but I don't believe it. He wants to bust our balls."

"Seems like the argument's personal between you and Johnson," I said.

He looked at me like I was an idiot. "He blew my friend's head off. Yeah, it's fucking personal."

"Before that. You came into the meeting looking for a fight."

"See this arm?" He extended his left arm across the desk. It had plenty of muscle on it. "Last summer he broke it."

"Looks like it's healed okay. What did you do to make him break it?"

Anger flashed across his face. "Nothing. I mind my own business."

I shook my head. "You mind your own business like last night when you threw the chair through the window?"

A mischievous smile played on his lips. "He deserved that."

"So why pay if you think he's going to keep busting you?"

He shrugged. "Maybe the money slows him down." Something in his voice sounded almost like hope.

"What's the business you were minding when he came into your neighborhood?"

"Nothing. Selling reefer. A little meth."

"Meth is nothing?"

"You ever see the fuckheads that buy it?"

"I see why he broke your arm."

"You want the money?"

"Not really." I picked up the bag. "Coins. No one wants you breaking into your piggy banks."

He sighed. "Do I leave the money?"

I shrugged. "Sure. Leave it."

He stood and headed to the door, but hesitated and turned back to me. "Two plus two isn't four with you either, right?"

I considered that. "To tell the truth, I'm not sure what it is."

He nodded. "Yeah. Me neither."

When he was gone, I unlocked the file cabinet drawer where I'd stashed the bottle of Jim Beam and the Baggie of coke. Either one would make my day happier. I dropped in the bag of money, closed the drawer, and locked it.

Then I put on my coat and headed for the door.

As I reached for the knob, someone knocked.

Maybe Rafael had changed his mind about the money. Maybe he hadn't saved enough for subway fare.

I opened the door. Bill Gubman, sitting in his wheelchair, stared up at me.

I invited him in, closed the door, and went back to my desk. My coat stayed on. His visit would be quick if I had any control over it.

His voice was calm, gentle, concerned. "Sooner or later we all step in shit. It's part of living."

I had no idea where he was heading, so I said, "Sure."

"But I've never seen anyone else dance in it the way you do."

I shrugged. "You heard about last night?"

"There were eyewitnesses at the construction site, Joe. One of them, a sixty-four-year-old woman who writes a column in a little paper called the *Pleasant Prairie News*, recognized you from TV coverage of the Southshore shootings. She said she was certain she saw you. She said you waved at her. Is that true, Joe? Did you wave?"

"I might have."

"Do you know how much trouble it takes to quiet down the Pleasant Prairie police and their beloved columnist?"

I shrugged. "How much?"

He gave me a tight-lipped smile. "Too much, as it turns out. They've put a warrant out for your arrest. The Chicago department will try to execute it."

"What are the charges?"

"Felony burglary, criminal damage to property, a little of this, and a little of that. You're looking at ten to twelve years in prison, so you'll be out in time to enjoy retirement."

"Are you taking me in?"

"Me? Hell, no. I'm giving you a heads-up."

"Thanks, I guess. What do you think I should do?"

"You might want to call your lawyer."

"Of course."

"And then you need to make yourself hard to find."

"You think?"

"You do if you want to stay in this investigation."

"I never wanted in to begin with."

"Right now you don't have a lot of choices. You either can stay out of sight and keep working or you can go to jail."

"How about putting my tail between my legs and hiding in a faraway corner where no one can find me?"

"That's a third choice, I guess, but as much as you talk about running away I don't see you doing it."

I had nothing to say to that. So I said, "Those FBI guys who saw us at Daley Plaza have been following me. They pulled me into a van yesterday and came by my house this morning. They want me to inform for them."

"What did you tell them?"

"I said I wanted total immunity."

Bill shook his head. "They'll never give it to you."

"That's what they said."

Bill smiled a little.

"Why don't you just pal up with them?" I said. "It would make your investigation easier and your life simpler. Mine too."

He shook his head. "There's a key difference between them and us. They want to expose Johnson's crew and all the ugly ways it ties to the department. They figure that'll clean up the city. We want to get rid of Johnson and his crew without exposing them. We figure that'll clean up the city too and also save a lot of heartache. The FBI wants headlines. We don't."

"I figure the FBI would call it justice, not headlines."

"They can call it what they like. If they bring this out in the open, everyone from the superintendent to the cop writing parking tickets suffers." He looked me in the eyes. "I prefer to do this quietly."

"You're taking a lot of risks to bury Johnson."

"He won't be the first bad cop the department has buried."

"That doesn't make me like it any better."

He stared at me over the desk for awhile. "Can I count on you?"

I shrugged. "Sure."

"I hear you're drinking again."

The comment felt like a test but I saw no reason to lie. "A little."

"That's a mistake—slippery slope and all that."

"How about you?" I said. "Can you drink with the pain meds?"

"Strictly prohibited."

"I don't suppose you want to get one, then," I said.

He gave me the smallest smile. "How about a cup of coffee?"

"You know how sad that is?"

He shrugged. "It's where we are."

I thought about that and shrugged too. "Sure, let's go."

We rode the elevator to the street. Bill had parked a police van in a no-parking zone in front of the building. He pulled out a set of keys attached to a remote unit and hit a button with his thumb. A side door panel slid open. He hit more buttons and an electric wheelchair lift dropped like a drawbridge and lowered to the sidewalk.

"Get in," he said.

I did, and, after the lift raised him into the van, he got himself behind the steering wheel and started the engine.

"Very impressive," I said.

He shifted the van hard into Drive. "I hate every moment of it."

As we pulled into traffic, I glanced toward the sidewalk. A man with a butterfly bandage on his face was staring at me through the windshield.

Raj.

He looked terrified that I'd gotten into a police van with a man some knew as my friend, more knew as the first police officer who'd gotten shot in my company, and every cop in the city knew as the new police liaison to the Chicago Board of Ethics—the man who would be most interested in destroying a group like Johnson's.

TWENTY-ONE

WE WENT TO THE Deluxe Diner on Harrison, and when we got back Bill dropped me off at my building. The afternoon sky had turned gray and weighed heavy on the city.

"Don't get picked up," Bill said.

"I'll try not to."

"You know where you're going to stay?"

"You want me to tell you?"

"Probably not. But check in, okay?"

I said I would.

His eyes got emotional. I'd seen that happen to other hard men who'd taken a bullet or come close to dying. Now and then, they teared up easily. Their voices choked in their throats. "Take care of yourself," he said.

"I'll try."

He pulled from the curb and I watched him go. I didn't know why but I felt like he'd given me a Judas kiss.

I rode the elevator to my office. The envelope of fake documents that Bill had given me sat in a file drawer. I got it out and put it in a canvas duffel bag. The duffel bag still had plenty of room. I put in the bottle of Jim Beam, the Baggie of coke, and the vinyl sack of money that Rafael had delivered. Then I rode the elevator back to the street and walked to my car.

A POLICE CRUISER WAS parked in front of my house. Two cops sat chatting in the front seat. They looked like they were on patrol and taking a break but I knew better. They undoubtedly had a copy of my arrest warrant. I drove past, went around the block, and parked in front of a three-flat that backed against my yard. A concrete path ran alongside the building. I took the path and hopped over the fence that separated the properties, then jogged across my yard, climbed the porch steps, and let myself in through the back door.

I left the lights off, went to my bedroom, pulled a suitcase from the closet, and loaded it with clothes and the stuff I kept in the bathroom medicine cabinet. I made a quick tour of the house and returned with some CDs, a couple of books, and my laptop. They went in on top of the clothes. I left my checkbook behind. Johnson had handed me a pile of cash when we'd sold the copper and transformers that we stole from the Wisconsin worksite. I went to the kitchen and looked around. I felt like taking a drawer and emptying the kitchen knives into my suitcase. I got a glass of water and left the drawer where it was. The Ruger .38 would be enough or it wouldn't.

Ten minutes after I came in through the back door, I went out again, unsure when I would return, or if.

I drove east on Montrose, cut through an underpass and

across Lake Shore Drive, and cruised into the lakefront park. A two-lane road curved around Montrose Harbor to a parking lot. I glided along the road, parked facing the gray water, got out, and walked toward the lake.

Waves swelled and sank as they approached the shore, then lipped up and splashed against the breakwater as if a storm had passed and the city was relaxing into peace. A single seagull floated forty yards off shore, rising and sinking on the waves. The sun was dipping behind the condo towers on the other side of the park. Long shadows from the leafless trees faded and disappeared into thicker, colder shadows.

I stared at the lake, watched the seagull rise and fall like the huge power of the lake was nothing, just a place to sit. When Corrine and I were married, she taught me to do breathing exercises when I came home so wound up that her fingers and lips couldn't reach me. Now I breathed in and breathed out, timing my breath to match the rise and fall of the seagull.

My body relaxed. My mind eased.

I breathed in and breathed out.

I closed my eyes, tried to let go.

The seagull disappeared and, sharp as daylight, Raj appeared in my mind. He stood on the sidewalk outside my office. He stared at me as I sat in Bill Gubman's police van. Alarm crossed his face.

"Damn," I said and opened my eyes. Raj had seen me with Bill. What would he do? If he ran to Johnson or Monroe, I was done. They would hit me hard—from behind, on the side, any way they could take me out for good. And why wouldn't Raj tell them? Because I'd pulled him off the barbed wire last night? Compared to the twenty-year stretch in prison that he would know Bill Gubman could give him, a couple of minutes in barbed wire was nothing.

But what if Raj didn't run to Johnson or Monroe? I would need to move fast. Bill had told me I needed to start spreading the bad rumors thick if I wanted Monroe to move against Johnson. That seemed right. If I got to Monroe before Raj did, I might confuse everyone so much that no one would know who to trust.

I pulled out my cell phone. Bill also had suggested I talk to my lawyer. He'd given me worse advice plenty of times. Larry's receptionist put my call through to his office, and he answered, "Where the hell are you?"

"At the beach," I said. "Pretty afternoon. Girls in bikinis. Sand between the toes."

He said nothing.

"Larry?"

"Are you drinking?"

"I wish."

"You're on TV again," he said. "They say you burglarized a processing plant."

"True."

"What the hell are you doing, Joe?"

"I'm trying to figure that out."

"I wouldn't always say this but you should turn yourself in. You killed a man and now you've got a warrant out for your arrest. A cop looking for a promotion might decide to shoot you and save the time at trial."

"Turning myself in is your best advice?"

"That or buy a ticket for Brazil."

"I've heard good things about Brazil. Food's better than in jail."

"So I've heard."

"Thanks, Larry." He'd given me nothing I could use but I couldn't blame him for that.

"What are you going to do, Joe?" He sounded genuinely concerned.

"Like I said, I'm trying to figure that out."

"As soon as you do, call me," he said.

I promised I would and we hung up.

I stood by the lake and watched the seagull until the cold air seeped through my jeans and jacket, then stood awhile longer. My watch said the time was 4:05. The sun would set in about half an hour. Mom had asked me to come for dinner at 7:00. With a warrant out for my arrest and a police cruiser parked in front of my house, going home wasn't an option. Going to my office was no better. A bar that I knew about cranked the heat and poured a deep enough shot to make it the warmest place on earth. But if I walked in the door I might stay forever. I went to my car, opened the trunk, and got out the bottle of Jim Beam. A long drink warmed my insides and made me shudder. It felt good. It also made me hate myself a little. I put the bottle away, got into the front seat, and started the engine. My Skylark was seventeen years old but the heater worked fine.

As the sun fell, I adjusted the seat all the way back and closed my eyes. For two hours, I drifted in and out of anxious dreams. I tried to picture myself in bed with Corrine but as I fell asleep she disappeared and a man hanging in barbed wire took her place. I tried to picture myself in bed with Lucinda, and she faded into a darkness where cops shot at each other. I tried Tina, the girl Raj offered me at The Spa Club. I imagined myself taking her from behind, imagined her yelling with pleasure as I fucked her but she disappeared too and I was alone and afraid.

MOM LIVED IN A yellow bungalow on West Leland. A tall, skinny white pine grew in the front corner of the yard. Ever since an October storm, the top third of the tree had tilted to the south like it knew enough to run but couldn't. Outside the front door, two boxwoods trimmed into little balls shimmered in the headlights as I pulled into the driveway.

I went around the side of the house, tapped on the back door, and let myself in. Mom stood at the stove, a small woman in blue jeans and a blue cotton work shirt. The house smelled of roasting meat and potatoes, with a sweet, sour edge of butter and onions. Mom stirred a pot of boiling broth. A plate of cooked pierogi stood on one side of the pot, a plate of uncooked pierogi on the other. The kitchen was warm, almost too comforting, and I resisted an impulse to back out of the house and run.

"I didn't think you would come," Mom said, her voice soft, her back to me.

"Of course I came," I said, soft too. "I told you I would."

She ladled the pierogi from the pot into a colander, turned to me. She screwed her lips to the side. "The police came by this afternoon. I'm supposed to call them if you're here."

I knew better than to ask but couldn't help myself. "Did you tell them I was coming this evening?"

The spoon dropped from her hand and clattered on the floor. She came to me and hugged me like a woman four times her size. When she was done, she let me go and said, "You should be ashamed." Her eyes were dry, her voice calm. She might have meant that I should be ashamed because I should have trusted her. She might have meant I should have avoided getting in trouble. She might have meant it all. I didn't ask.

I pointed my thumb at the door to the living room, where Mom's television was on, and said, "Is Jason in there?"

The faintest of smiles formed on her lips and she nodded. "Go see him."

Jason was lying on the couch. He was wearing blue flannel pajamas. I thought I recognized them. I'd worn pajamas that looked like them when I was eleven years old.

"Hey," I said, trying to put cheer into my voice.

"Hey," he said. He kept his eyes on the television.

"How're you feeling?"

Eyes still on the television. "Fine."

I looked at the screen. Jennifer Grey was tangoing with Patrick Swayze in *Dirty Dancing*. Not the kind of movie Jason normally watched.

"That any good?"

He shrugged, gestured toward the kitchen. "She won't let me watch the news."

"Since when do you watch the news?" I said.

"Since you're on it." His eyes stayed on the television.

I picked up the remote from the table next to him and punched the power button. Jennifer Grey disappeared into a pinpoint of light. Jason still looked at the screen.

I stepped between him and the television, stooped, and looked at him eye to eye. "It's going to be all right."

"Of course it is," he said. He didn't believe it for a second. He gestured again toward the kitchen. "She said it would be too."

I showed him my palms. "You think we're lying?"

"I think you don't know." A smart eleven-year-old.

"You're right, but I'm doing everything I can to make it okay."

"Like committing a robbery?"

"I didn't—" I stopped. He deserved the truth and I wished I knew it. "It's complicated," I said. "You've got to trust me."

He looked at me for awhile, then said, "Why?"

"Because—" I started. "Just because."

"That's not a reason."

"I know. But it's all I've got."

He nodded unhappily. "Now can I watch TV?"

I shook my head. "Where did you get those pajamas?"

He tipped his head toward the kitchen.

"Mom?" I called.

She came to the door.

I pointed at Jason and asked, "Are those—?"

She nodded. "Your old pajamas."

"You've saved them for thirty-five years?"

"They were in perfectly good shape."

"But thirty-five years?"

"I thought maybe one day I would have a grandson."

"If you did, I would buy him pajamas myself."

She turned back to the kitchen. "They were in perfect shape."

Fifteen minutes later, Mom called us to the table. She'd served enough food to feed twelve—a platter of roasted pork, pierogi sautéed with onions, a bowl of mashed potatoes, red cabbage salad, sliced and buttered bread. Jason was half my size and usually ate twice as much as I did but tonight he ate slowly, carefully, chewing each bite far longer than he needed to. Mom watched him, concerned.

"Still uncomfortable to eat?" I asked him.

He shook his head.

Mom said, "The doctor says he's fine with a regular diet." She spooned potatoes onto his already full plate.

"Can I be done?" he said.

"Eat your dinner first," Mom said.

He cut a small bite of pork, put it in his mouth, chewed a long time, then raised his napkin to his mouth and spit the pork into it. He slid his chair away from the table and wandered back into the living room. A few moments later, he turned on *Dirty Dancing*.

Mom stared at his plate, then looked at me. "Eat *your* dinner, for God's sake."

I did.

Afterward, I went to the living room and sat next to Jason on the couch. He was quiet and I kept my mouth shut, and after a little while he leaned against me and I put my arm around his shoulder and held him. We stayed like that for an hour, maybe more. Then Mom came in and said Jason should get some sleep.

I squeezed his shoulder and said, "Get well fast."

He nodded and said, "I want to go back to your house with you."

"Soon, okay?" I said. "Real soon."

I DROVE TO THE Patio Motel, a blue two-story strip with a big 1960s-style neon sign out front, left over from when Lincoln Avenue was a main route in and out of the city for trucks and tourists. Now the customers were mostly men and women who'd slipped away from their famlies and parked their cars side by side outside rooms with a single dim light on or none at all. A shoulder-high wooden fence blocked the parking lot from the street. I parked close to it to make my Skylark invisible—or almost—and went into the office.

The man behind the desk was bald and pronounced his *R*s like *W*s. He took my fifty-five dollars and gave me a room key. If he recognized me from the TV news, he didn't show it.

The room had a NO SMOKING sign on the door and smelled like stale smoke. The walls could have used painting, the floors a new carpet, but the bed looked just right. I put my suitcase on a chair next to it, went back to the door and chained it, then peered out the window at the traffic and the nighttime city. The business next door advertised yoga tai-chi. Out front, the block-lettered Patio Motel sign glowed orange against the dark. Under the name of the motel, blue neon cursive added, AN ADVENTURE IN LIVING. If that wasn't enough, another sign offered free movies.

I pulled the curtains, stripped off my pants and shirt, turned off the light, and climbed into bed. The unfamiliar darkness and smells surrounded me. The bedside clock said the time was 10:28. I flipped the lamp back on and fished my cell phone out of my jeans. Corrine had told me she would come to me if I needed her. Did I need her? I dialed her home number. It rang four times and her machine picked up. I listened to her voice asking me to leave a message but hung up before the recording signal. I dialed her cell phone. It rang six times and put me through to voice mail. I hung up again.

I turned off the lamp and stretched out in the strange bed. I spun David Russo's ring on my finger. Where would Corrine be at this time of night? That kind of thinking would get me nowhere, so I thought about Lucinda, then Mom, and then Jason. Jason had told me that he wanted to go home. I thought about that. My house was his home. I was his home. That made me glad, and I wondered if that was a good thing. Good or bad didn't matter, I decided—it just made me glad. I realized I wanted to go home too.

TWENTY-TWO

I WOKE EARLY. THE bedside clock said 5:34. The sun wouldn't come up for another hour.

I showered and shaved, then stepped out into the morning cold and darkness and dropped the room key at the front desk. A box at the corner sold copies of the *Chicago Tribune*. I dropped in my quarters and looked at the paper under a streetlight. It had a photo of me at the bottom of the front page. The photo was old, taken around the time the police department fired me after I crashed my cruiser. I looked drunk in the photo. No surprise. I had more hair then, less of it gray. I had a cut on my chin. You would still recognize me.

At the corner a block and a half away, the lights were on in a diner. I walked to it and went inside. A TV played near the ceiling. The air was warm and smelled like bacon grease. The griddle was out in the open, and the griddle man—a dark-haired kid in white pants, white T-shirt, and white apron—welcomed me with a big smile as I sat at the counter. Maybe he hadn't read the paper.

He said he cooked the best hash browns in the city, so I told him to give me some with a couple of scrambled eggs, toast, and sausage. A woman came in wearing a short blue skirt, scuffed red high heels, a leather jacket, and dirty blond hair that needed a brush. She sat two stools away from me and eyed me like I might be business, then told the griddle man she wanted coffee. He didn't offer her hash browns but poured her a cup and slid a container of sugar across the counter to her. She used four packs.

Breakfast did me good. The hooker watched me eat. So did the griddle man.

"How're the hash browns?" he said.

"Best in the city."

He nodded his appreciation. "My secret recipe," he said.

The hooker frowned. "He uses boric acid. Also kills roaches."

He grabbed a dirty dishtowel and threw it at her. "Get the fuck out of my restaurant."

She rolled her eyes like she'd heard that before. "Give me more coffee."

He did.

The six A.M. news came on and an anchorwoman with dark hair and dark eyes said that a tanker truck full of petroleum had flipped on the Southside and was burning. She cut away to a reporter standing at the crash site. The camera showed huge flames rising from the truck into the dark sky. Firemen stood at a distance, aiming hoses at the edges of the fire, controlling the burn, not fighting it. You could just about feel waves of heat coming off the TV.

The griddle man looked at the screen and shook his head. "Like hell itself is burning."

The hooker shrugged.

The on-site reporter finished his story and cut back to the anchorwoman. She shook her head like she felt the heat too, then said, "Meanwhile, police continue their search for—"

I gulped another bite of toast, took a ten-dollar bill from my wallet, and tossed it on the counter. I scurried for the door as a picture of me popped onto the screen. The griddle man watched me like I'd turned into a strange, dangerous animal. The hooker didn't seem to notice me go.

AT 6:45, THE STREETS near my office were busy with delivery trucks unloading boxes of office supplies, loaves of bread, and cases of canned soft drinks. I pulled my car to the curb and watched. Classes at the secretarial school started at 8:00. Roselle Turner usually showed up to open the doors around 7:00. I pulled out the *Tribune* and waited.

The front-page article said the police had issued a warrant for my arrest and were keeping an eye on the places I was known to frequent. It said I might have left the city and so the police had issued a multistate alert too. It described the theft at the processing plant and the witness account of me there. It said I was likely armed and should be considered dangerous.

I had the Ruger holstered on my side. But dangerous? I figured I was mostly dangerous to myself.

The article continued on page eight. It retold the events at Southshore Village and gave the highlights of my record as a cop and private investigator. According to the reporter, I was a good guy who'd gone bad. Nothing I didn't know already. I tossed the paper onto the passenger seat.

At 6:56 Roselle Turner walked past my car. I waited five minutes, then dialed 411, asked for the number to the secretarial school, and dialed again. She picked up, breathless, like she'd run for the phone.

"Hi, Roselle," I said. "It's Joe Kozmarski."

"Jesus! What do *you* want?" So much for flirting.

"A favor. Will you look in the hall and tell me if anyone's near my office door?"

"You mean like a policeman?"

I sighed. "Yes."

"I don't need to look in the hall. There's one at your door and another at the elevators. Both in uniforms. Your door is open. I think more of them are inside, taking your office apart by the sound of it."

That quieted me.

She got polite but with a sarcastic edge, as if I'd let her down personally. "Would you like me to let them know you're looking for them?"

"I would like you to—" I started.

"Yes?"

"Forget it. Thanks, Roselle."

She hung up.

The police had blocked off my house. They'd visited Mom. They were searching my office. Where could I go? Corrine hadn't answered her phone last night. Maybe the police had visited her too. Maybe they'd told her that if she helped me or took me in, she'd become an accessory after the fact. Or maybe no one had visited her. Maybe she'd decided on her own to cut me off.

Lucinda might still be safe. The police knew about my connections with her and would have talked with her, but she knew how to shake them if they were watching her and she could help me hide if I needed her to. Sooner or later, I figured, I would need that—maybe tonight if I needed a place to sleep and didn't want to show myself to the eyes of another motel owner. But not yet.

I started my car and drove north through the Loop, up Michigan Avenue, and along the lakefront to The Spa Club. Some guys like sex at night. Some guys like it in the morning. Some like it all day long. I figured the club would be open.

The valet took my car, and the elevator gave me a ride to the top floor. I carried the vinyl bag of cash and coins that Rafael had delivered to my office. Stuffed into my inside jacket pocket were phony bank receipts that Bill Gubman had given me, showing that Johnson had skimmed profits from his crew.

In the blue-lighted lounge, three men—two in suits and ties, one in exercise clothes—sat at tables eating breakfast. They'd probably told their wives they had early morning meetings and had come to the club to start their day right. The hostess who'd been working when Monroe, Raj, and Finley had brought me to the club the first time was on duty again. She recognized me and offered me a table.

I shook my head. "Is Bob Monroe around?"

Her look told me I could relax, take off my shoes, slip off my underwear, stay awhile. "He just came in." She put a hand on my elbow and guided me to a table. "Sit down and I'll see if he's available."

I sat and waited.

Tina, the Russian girl Raj had offered me, came in wearing a little black outfit. She looked like she'd been working all night. She still looked good. She saw me and gave me a big smile like we were old friends. "Good morning!" she said brightly.

"'Morning," I said.

She came to my table. "What can I do for you?" she said.

"I already ate."

She laughed. I'd misunderstood her offer. "If you want, we could go into the back," she said.

Bob Monroe came into the room from a door behind the hostess desk. When Tina saw him heading for my table, she said, "Maybe later?"

"Right," I said.

Monroe smiled and raised his eyebrows like he approved. "'Morning," he said. "You want to talk?"

We went back through the door he'd come from. There were two offices—Johnson's on the right, Monroe's on the left—and a third room, with a conference table, at the end of the hall. Johnson was sitting at a desk in his office, talking on the phone, his chair swiveled away from the door. We went into Monroe's office.

"You know there's a warrant out for you?" Monroe said. "We thought someone might have picked you up by now. Johnson thought you'd already be trading information about us in return for empty promises."

I dropped the vinyl bag onto the desk and sat. "I'm still free," I said, "and I don't trade information. You should know that by now."

He nodded and sat at the desk. "I do know it. Johnson's harder to convince." He eyed the vinyl bag. "What's that?"

I shrugged. "First weekly payment from Rafael."

His eyes lighted up. "You're kidding. That knucklehead said he wouldn't pay. What did you do?"

"Nothing," I said. "He walked into my office and offered me the money."

"Yeah, right." He laughed. "Whatever you did, I'm impressed." He leaned so he could see out his door and across the hall. "Hey, Earl, you've got to see this."

After a moment, Johnson stepped into the office. If he was surprised to see me, he didn't show it.

Monroe gestured at the vinyl bag. "Look what the cat dragged in." He grinned like he'd scored a point against Johnson. "He got it from Rafael."

Johnson glanced at me, then picked up the bag. He unzipped it and poured the bills and change onto the desk. The bills were crumpled, a lot of tens and fives and ones. The coins included nickels and pennies. "What the hell is that?" he said.

"First weekly payment," I said. "A few days early."

Johnson shook his head. "Tell him next time you want it in twenties and fifties. You're not collecting milk money."

He left the office, went into his own, and closed the door behind him.

Monroe still grinned. "Some guys are hard to please."

I reached and closed his door, then pulled out the pile of phony receipts and put them on the desk next to the money.

He stared at my eyes. "What's that?" he said.

"Take a look."

As he read the receipts, his face angered. "You're full of surprises this morning. Where'd you get these?"

"I was looking into you guys long before the night at Southshore."

"That doesn't answer my question."

I said, "I was following Johnson and saw what he was up to. I saw him going into the banks. If you want bank records as a cop, you go to a judge. If I want them, I go to a friend."

He looked at the receipts and shook his head, disgusted. Then he picked up his phone, pushed a button, and a moment later said, "Is Raj here? Send him in."

Sweat broke between my shoulders. If Raj told Monroe that he saw me with Bill Gubman, my game would be over.

A minute later, Raj tapped on the office door and stepped inside. He was wearing a jacket like he'd just come in from the cold. He looked like he hadn't slept. His face fell when he saw me. He turned to Monroe. "Cindi said you wanted to see me."

Monroe tossed the receipts onto the desk and Raj picked them up. Raj looked at them like he was trying to figure out what he was seeing, trying to make sense of it. Then he said to Monroe, "Where did you get these?"

Monroe nodded at me, grim faced. "Joe did some private work. What do you make of them?"

Raj looked at me long, without expression, and I figured this was it—he would tell Monroe that he'd seen me with Bill, they would call Johnson into the office, and then someone would get hurt or worse. I figured that someone would be me. The Ruger rested against my side and I wondered if I had enough energy to reach for it when the moment came.

Raj turned to Monroe. "That fucking Johnson!" he said.

Monroe nodded.

I almost laughed. I looked at Raj, hoping he would give me a glance, a gesture, that told me we were in this together.

He kept his eyes on Monroe. "What now?"

Monroe thought. "It's an opportunity," he said.

Raj thought so too and nodded.

"I'll call a meeting for tonight," Monroe said. "Let's make sure everyone's there." He turned to me. "It's an opportunity for you too."

"Yeah?"

"Yeah," he said. "We're going to make some changes around here."

I shook my head. "I've known Johnson since he started at the department. He's tough—you don't want to underestimate him."

Monroe waved that away. "I've seen what he can do and I know who he is. But you know what? He shits out of the same hole I do. And right now"—Monroe allowed himself a little smile—"he's deep in it."

I shrugged. "Can I have the receipts?"

"No," he said and held his hand toward Raj, who gave them to him. Monroe folded them and stuck them into a pocket. "Right now we need them."

Raj and I left the office together and walked into the lounge. It was empty. The men had finished their breakfasts. The hostess was gone from her desk, probably in a back room with one of the men.

I stopped Raj. "Why are you helping me? Why didn't you tell Monroe?"

"Tell him what?"

"I know you saw me yesterday."

He glanced at the empty lounge. "This whole thing is about to come down, isn't it?"

I nodded, said, "Maybe."

He thought about that and looked defeated. He said, "I don't know what you're up to. But when it comes down, you're going to say I did the right thing, okay?"

"Yeah," I said. "I'll do that."

TWENTY-THREE

I SPENT THE MORNING driving around the city in Raj's SUV. Raj said every patrolman in the city knew about my Skylark, down to the scratches on the bumpers, so my car stayed in the parking garage fourteen floors below The Spa Club.

I cruised for awhile through the side streets near my house. The sun was burning through the clouds. The light played off the last leaves hanging on the tree branches and glared off the windshields of parked cars.

At 9:30, I called Lucinda. "Hey," she said when she heard my voice. "Is this your one call from jail?"

"Not yet," I said. "Have the police been there?"

"Still here—parked on the street. Last night they came in and tried to sweet-talk me into helping them find you."

"What did you tell them?"

"I offered them coffee and talked sweet to them too."

"Yeah?"

"So they stopped the sweet talk and threatened me with

everything in the book and a little that they made up. They seemed to forget that I used to be a cop. I threatened them back and kicked them out of my apartment, and now they're sitting outside in the cold."

"Can you slip away from them?"

"Are you kidding? Where do you want to meet?"

I told her and added, "Bring a pen and paper."

"You going to write your last will and testament?"

"Something like that."

"I'll see you in a little bit," she said.

"Hey, how was dinner with Peter Finley?"

"He spent the whole time trying to convince me to work at The Spa Club. He said selling me as an ex-cop would bring in big money. Guys would like that, girls too if I was willing. He said I could make five times what I made in the department."

"I believe it. Did you find out anything useful?"

"Nothing new. He's got little love for Bob Monroe, less for Raj, and none at all for you. I think he's got ambitions to replace Monroe as number two, behind Johnson."

"Anything else?"

"No, he was too busy looking down my shirt and putting his hand on my thigh."

"At least he's got good taste. When are you going out again?"

"Not funny," she said.

Next I called Corrine. She answered on the third ring and sounded like I'd woken her.

"Hi," I said.

She was quiet, then asked, "Where are you?" She said it like she wasn't sure she wanted to know.

"Driving around."

That was enough of an answer. "They've got you on the news. And in the papers." She sounded as if she was holding back tears.

"I know."

"Are you going to turn yourself in?"

"No," I said. "Do you think I should?"

"I don't know." Then, "Are you going to come over here?"

"No," I said again. "Not right now."

We were both quiet for awhile. She said, "Why did you call?"

Because I'd wanted to hear her voice. Because I'd wanted to ask where she'd been last night. I said, "To tell you I love you."

She said nothing to that.

"Corrine?"

She said, "I love you too, Joe, but I don't know if I love you *this* much."

At 10:30, I walked into the Lincoln Park Conservatory, a four-room greenhouse that looked like an enormous glass-roofed pagoda. A concrete path snaked through gardens of ferns and tropical flowers, under palm trees, past hanging baskets of orchids, and past an artificial waterfall. The air was warm and moist—the weather from a tropical rainforest. Lucinda was sitting on a bench under a palm tree.

I sat next to her.

"It's nice here," she said.

I nodded. "I'm thinking of taking off my clothes and swimming in the waterfall."

"I can see the headlines now."

"Any trouble getting away from your apartment?" I asked.

She smiled. "I left the cruiser boxed in at a stoplight two blocks from my place."

"You're good," I said.

She looked me in the eyes. "Yes."

"Did you bring the pen and paper?"

She reached into a brown leather bag and handed them to me.

I told her about the meeting that Monroe was scheduling for the evening, and, as I did, I drew a sketch of The Spa Club.

The sketch showed the front lounge with the hostess desk, the hallway that extended behind the desk, and the two offices and the conference room that the hallway led to. I drew another hallway too, which led to a lobby and then the back rooms where you could get anything that money could buy, the room with television monitors, and the door to the emergency exit at the end of that hallway. I put an X on the conference room and another on the emergency exit. The meeting where Monroe confronted Johnson would happen in the conference room, I figured. If Lucinda was willing to take the risk, I wanted her to get into the building and up to the fourteenth floor, and to be standing in the stairwell outside the emergency exit when the meeting started.

I said, "I can think of about a dozen ways this meeting could blow up. If it does, I wouldn't mind having backup—the more the better. Drive a tank up the stairs if you can. Or at least bring a couple guns and be ready to use them."

Lucinda studied the diagram. "Do any of the TV monitors show the stairwell?"

"Not that I noticed," I said, "but I'll check. If there's a camera, I'll disable it. If I can't, I'll call and tell you not to come."

"Do they have guards?"

I shook my head. "Not when they're open for business. They probably figure it would wreck the mood."

"They'll be open this evening?"

"They're always open."

"Is there anything else that could stop me between the emergency exit and the meeting room?"

I thought about Tina, who'd offered herself to me twice. I thought about the women at the hostess desk. "Nothing you can't brush aside."

She put the paper and pen in her bag.

Then I told her about the conversation I'd had with Raj after we left Monroe's office.

"Can you count on him to stay quiet?"

I shook my head. "He's one of the ways this could blow up. He's seriously spooked. Odds are equal that he keeps his mouth shut or tells everything to Monroe."

"Of if he figures Monroe is a lost cause, he could run to Johnson," Lucinda said.

I thought about that. "Could be, but so far he's always stood by Monroe. Finley seems to be Johnson's closest friend. The other guys, I don't know. Monroe expects them to line up behind him when he shows that Johnson's been ripping them off."

Footsteps approached on the concrete path. Lucinda and I shut our mouths and gazed up at the yellow fruit that hung in clusters from a palm tree. Gray light filtered through the foggy glass above the tree. More footsteps approached from the other side.

Stuart Felicano, the lead FBI agent, stepped into view on one side. The bridge of his nose was bruised where I'd hit him. But he wore a pressed blue suit and looked like he'd gotten a good night's sleep. Felicano's heavyset partner stepped into view on the other side, also in a suit. There was nowhere to run.

I looked at Lucinda.

She shook her head, her eyes stunned. "Jesus! I'm sorry. I didn't think anyone—"

"Good morning, Mr. Kozmarski," Felicano said. "You look surprised to see us."

"No more than if you'd swung in on vines."

He smiled. "Do you have a moment to talk?"

"Do I have a choice?"

Still smiling. "We met with your friend Bill Gubman this morning."

"Yeah?"

"Yeah. He seems to be under the mistaken impression that he can make Earl Johnson's crew disappear. No arrests. No trials. No scandal. He wants to bury them in an unmarked grave."

"I wouldn't know about that."

His smile broadened. "So, that made us wonder about you. You're at the Southshore shooting. You're seen stealing from another site in Wisconsin. You're working with Johnson's crew. There's a warrant out for your arrest. But you're also hanging out with Gubman. He might be an old friend but he looks like the last guy you'd want to be found with. So what's between him and you?"

"What did he say?"

"He said he wouldn't know about you."

"Makes sense. Most of the time I don't even know about myself."

His smile fell hard from his face. "Don't be that way."

I shrugged. "I don't think I can help you."

"You're wrong," he said. "You could help a lot. Have you learned anything more about Johnson?"

Other than that he was about to fall off a wall? I shook my head. "Nothing."

"What about Farid el Raj?"

"What about him?"

"We hear he might be making a play on Johnson for control of the crew."

Unless a lot more was happening than I knew, they'd heard wrong or gotten Raj mixed up with Monroe. "Are you listening to them on a wire?"

The other agent said, "That's none of your—"

Felicano patted the air to quiet him. "No wires," he said. "Johnson's planted as much sound equipment in his time as we have. We wouldn't get away with it."

"That makes hearing things hard."

"We still hear them."

The other agent said, "So what about el Raj?"

"I don't know about him either."

Felicano shook his head. "You're making a big mistake."

"Welcome to my life."

Two women in their sixties came down the path, talking about bromeliads. They wore dresses and canvas hats, like they were on a safari. One had a camera hanging around her neck. The FBI agents stepped aside and let them through.

When they'd passed, one of the agents said, "We could take you in on the warrant."

I agreed. "You could."

He tipped his head toward Lucinda. "We could take her in as accessory."

Lucinda held her wrists toward him like he might want to cuff them. "You could."

Felicano said, "Or we could leave you out on the street and see what happens. Guys like you don't live long."

"Whatever you prefer," I said, like he'd offered me a choice between white meat or dark.

My attitude didn't fool him. "I've dealt with guys like you before," he said. "You can work with us and come out a little dirtied but alive. Or you can do it alone with one chance in a hundred of coming out clean, ninety-nine chances of coming out dead or filthy. I'd think the choice would be easy. But guys like you take that one chance. I don't think you're courageous and I don't think you're just a bad gambler. I think you're afraid, scared to death of just getting by if getting by means compromising a little. Guys like you make no sense to me but that's what I think."

I tried a smile. "You nailed me."

He shook his head again, disappointed, maybe disgusted. "One chance in a hundred. Is it worth it?"

I shrugged. "Sure."

He shook his head again. "We'll be keeping our eyes on you," he said.

"That's reassuring," I said.

He looked at me like I was being a smart-ass, but with the trouble I was in I realized I might mean it.

When they were gone, Lucinda and I sat together for awhile without talking. A siren passed outside, then was quiet, and the city was far away.

Lucinda said, "Could Raj be up to something?"

"No," I said and thought about it some. "No."

Behind us, water dripped from a pipe near the ceiling onto a hard surface. The waterfall trickled down an artificial stone face and collected in a basin.

TWENTY-FOUR

I DROVE NORTH AND bought a hot dog at Byron's, then cruised for forty minutes looking for a place to park and eat. I went south and west and drove across Blackhawk Street until it dead-ended at the North Branch of the Chicago River. Five unofficial parking spots faced a thin strip of grass with leafless trees and then the river. One of the spots was open. I slid Raj's SUV into it. The hot dog was cold.

When I finished eating, I tilted the seat back, closed my eyes, and thought about the mess I'd gotten myself into. I had plenty of time to think and plenty to think about. Too much time and too much to think about. I tilted the seat up again and watched the river.

The sunlight glinted off the tree branches. The river moved so slow you would never know it moved at all.

In the summer, now and then, a heron would stand on the banks looking for a meal. I'd never seen one catch a fish. Supposedly an eagle or two had tested the air above the water. But on a cold sunny afternoon in November no birds stood on the grass, flew in the air, or perched in the brown branches, not even a sparrow.

In the 1990s, when most of the factories closed, fish swam back into the lower reaches of the river. The EPA forced the remaining factories to treat their waste before dumping it and to put toxic chemicals into metal drums and ship them to a dumpsite in Indiana. A river advocacy group got excited and started imagining bass jumping in the shallows and beavers building dams in the shadows of the old smokestacks. They convinced the city to dredge the chemical waste off the river bottom. Except the dredged chemicals clouded the water and the fish that had returned went belly up and washed onto the riverbanks.

That made me think. Was Felicano right? Was I so set on shoveling the dirt out of my life that I'd moved into a dirt pit? Did I need to climb out and keep living, knowing that I would never get completely clean?

I called Lucinda. When she picked up her phone, I said, "Am I obsessed with making things turn out the way they never can be?"

"Well, yeah," she said like it was obvious.

"Is that bad?"

"I don't know. Maybe."

AT 4:45, I DROVE back to The Spa Club. Rush-hour traffic filled the streets. Cars inched toward intersections with men and women strapped into their seats as if a sudden catastrophe might lift them out of the gridlock and hurtle them through the air.

At LaSalle and Division, a traffic cop held his hand up and

stopped me so that cross traffic could move through the inter-section. He stared through the windshield like he recognized me, and sweat beaded between my shoulder blades and on the insides of my legs. But he waved me through with the rest of the cars.

The valet at The Spa Club building took the keys to Raj's SUV and welcomed me by name. "Good afternoon, Mr. Koz-marski," he said. I was coming up in the world. Or going down.

The elevator man greeted me by name too and took me to the fourteenth floor.

The lounge was crowded. I waved hello to the hostess and cut past the tables. Men and women—mostly men—relaxed with drinks, wearing clothes that would be fine at the office if they put back on their ties or buttoned a couple more buttons on their blouses. Spa Club staff mingled with the customers, making small talk, flirting, moving on if the customers weren't interested. A man in a suit sat at a table with three other men in shirtsleeves. I thought I recognized the one in the suit from TV, forecasting the weather or making political promises. A waitress sat on his leg and he told her a joke that I couldn't hear, and the other men laughed but she just blushed, which must have taken some effort after working here. A woman dressed in black sat alone at a table in a corner, glaring at every-one else in the room. I wondered who she was waiting for and what she was doing at the club.

No one seemed to be heading toward the hall leading to the back rooms. Maybe that happened later in the evening after the drinks and small talk.

I went alone into the second lobby and into the back hall. The meeting with Johnson would start at 7:00 and Lucinda would climb the stairs to the fourteenth-floor emergency exit a half hour earlier.

No one was around, so I went to the monitor room, knocked once, and opened the door.

Peter Finley sat in a swivel chair with headphones on. Ten screens were on. Six showed rooms where the girls and boys who worked at The Spa Club took clients. Three of the rooms had clients in them now. The seventh screen showed the back door into the alley behind the building; the eighth, which was hazy, the front entrance. The ninth, which I hadn't noticed before, showed the front lounge and the elevator. The last I also hadn't noticed. It showed a stairwell. I figured the camera must be outside the emergency exit door.

Damn, I thought, but I grinned and said, "You always have someone in here watching and listening?"

Finley took off the earphones. "Twenty-four seven," he said. "We can't afford not to. Plus sitting in here beats the hell out of watching *Oprah*."

The meeting would start in just over two hours. In that time, I needed to disable the stairwell camera or the monitor that it fed, and I needed to do it in a way that looked like an electrical or mechanical malfunction, not like someone had damaged it on purpose. If the camera was still working, Lucinda would walk into the hands of Johnson's crew for a second time in three nights. This time, I figured, no one would walk her politely to her car. She would get hurt, and I would too.

"How are you liking the work?" Finley said.

I shrugged. "Beats sitting at home watching *Oprah*."

He gave that an uncommitted smile. "You know, when Earl

Johnson invited me to join his crew, I was like you. I resisted. I'd been doing some solo shit, taking a few bucks off the hookers who were standing on the corner and, if they were carrying a little crack, taking that too. Solo treated me just fine, I thought. But Earl had bigger plans and he convinced me. He also got me to clean myself up. No more crack. Now I'm having the time of my life."

I raised an imaginary glass. "Here's to Earl."

He considered that. "To tell the truth, he doesn't like you."

I dropped the imaginary glass and smiled. "Then fuck Earl, right?"

His half smile remained. "He's usually got good judgment about people."

I shrugged again and looked at the screens that showed the rooms with clients.

In one, a good-looking man I'd seen tending bar was sucking off a nude, balding fat man who looked like he was in his fifties. A woman—also nude, also fat, also in her fifties—sat in a chair a few feet away, watching the two men. She looked bored. I figured she was the fat man's wife.

In the second room, a man, also in his fifties but thin and well-muscled, was having sex with a big-breasted woman in her thirties I'd also seen around the club. The sex was tender, almost loving, and I wondered why they were here instead of in a bedroom at his home or a hotel room where no one could see them.

In the third room, two men were screwing Tina. One stood behind her and the other faced her mouth.

Finley caught me staring at the screen. He laughed. "You like that?"

I said nothing. I wanted to go to the room and slug the men.

"Tina's the best we've got," Finley said. "She'll do anything. Anything and anyone. She makes more in a day than some of the girls make in a week."

Why did I think she needed me to help? When I'd turned her down, she'd looked like I'd insulted her. Still, I wanted to beat up the men she was with. I also wanted to beat up Finley. I said, "You need to figure out how to install debit card machines on the girls so they vibrate for thirty seconds every time you add cash."

Finley looked puzzled.

"I'll see you later," I said and stepped into the hallway, closed the door behind me.

The hallway was still empty. I waited a moment, then turned to the emergency exit. The sooner the camera stopped working, the better.

As I reached for the door, a voice at the other end of the hall said, "Hey, Joe, I've been looking for you."

I turned, unsure how I would explain myself. Bob Monroe had come into the hallway from the lobby. He'd changed into brown warm-up pants and a matching hooded sweatshirt. Comfortable clothes for taking over the world. "Hey," I said, "what's up?"

"Come on." He nodded toward the front of the club. "We need to talk."

I followed him to the lounge, down the hall behind the hostess desk, and into his office.

He sat at his desk. "What were you doing back there?"

"I was going to cut the cables to the security camera so my friends could sneak in without paying."

He laughed but still wanted to know. "What were you doing?"

I shrugged. "Looking around. I like to know a place well, especially if I'm facing down someone like Johnson."

He nodded thoughtfully. "Good idea." Then he waved an open palm over his desk like he wanted to sell it to me. "What do you think?"

He'd spread the bank receipts that I'd given him across the desktop. Under each of them, he'd placed a couple more sheets of paper. Photocopies of police reports.

I picked up a receipt and a report. The report described an unsolved burglary of a construction site on the Northwest side. It was dated September 10 and said the burglary had occurred the previous night. It said twenty-four thousand dollars' worth of copper and other metals had been taken. The bank receipt also was dated September 10 and was for seven thousand dollars, a little less than a third of the value of the metal.

I picked up another receipt and report and saw the same pattern—an August 29 account of a sixteen-thousand-dollar burglary on the night of the 28th, and an August 29 bank receipt for four thousand, seven hundred and fifty dollars.

A third receipt and report showed the same, except the deposit occurred the day after the report.

"Wow," I said. "Where did you get the reports?"

Monroe looked at me sideways. "I'm a cop," he said. "Where do you think I got them?"

I looked over the papers on the desk. Monroe had done impressive work in lining up the information that could bring down Johnson. Bill Gubman had done impressive work in rigging the bank receipts so they would line up with the reports. "You think this will be enough to convince everyone?"

"I think so. Figuring that a couple of the construction sites overreported their losses, the bank total comes to about thirty percent of the value of the thefts. That's roughly the same percentage we get when we deal with our buyer."

I nodded, impressed again.

"I also checked the dates of the burglaries against the nights when our crew was working. No overlap. And I checked the dates against the work log. Johnson was off duty. He was on his own. I remember two of the dates in August. He said he was going out of town."

"Looks like you've got him."

He allowed himself a small smile. Then he said, "You should present the evidence tonight."

I shook my head. "Why me?"

He numbered the reasons on the thumb and first three fingers of his left hand. "You found the bank receipts. You're an outsider. No one thinks you've got anything against Johnson. And the guys all know Johnson and I have gone at it before and they'll be suspicious of anything I say." He touched his pinky. "Common sense. You present the evidence and then I step in."

If that was common sense, I didn't want any of it. "What happens to him after we show that he's been ripping you off?"

Monroe looked down at the desk and arranged the receipts and reports into neat piles. "He disappears."

I felt the ice in those words. Bill Gubman had told me about Victor Lopez, the kid who'd disappeared when he'd started talking too loud about the trouble Monroe was giving him.

Nothing had been found of the kid, Bill had said, not even a bone fragment.

"How does he disappear?" I said.

Monroe looked me in the eyes with the mild smile. "I do a little magic."

I knew better than to ask more. "You bury him?"

He said nothing.

"Sink him in the lake?"

Monroe said, "If you bury or sink him, he hasn't disappeared, has he? Someone comes along with a shovel or a storm shakes him off the lake bottom, and you've got yourself a big problem."

"How do you make it happen?"

His smile broadened.

Before he could tell me, there was a knock at the door.

He lifted a finger to tell me to hold on for a moment and said, "Yeah?"

The door opened and Finley stepped in. He held a Glock that looked a lot like mine but bigger. He pointed the gun at Monroe. Three other cops from Johnson's crew stepped in beside him. One of them was Raj. One of the others held a second gun, which he pointed at me.

"What the fuck is this?" said Monroe.

"Stand up," said Finley.

I stood.

"No," said Monroe.

Finley went around the desk and held his gun to Monroe's head. "Get up," he said. He couldn't have been calmer.

Monroe stood.

Finley patted him down, found nothing on him, and then removed a pistol from his desk drawer.

The other guy with the gun took my Ruger out of my over-the-shoulder rig and handed it to Finley.

I tried to catch Raj's eyes. He wasn't looking at me.

I said to Monroe, "What's going on?"

Monroe looked unhappy. "We just got fucked," he said.

TWENTY-FIVE

THE GUY WHO'D TAKEN my gun stuck his head out of the
door and looked toward the hostess desk to make sure no one
was watching. Then Finley hurried us into the hallway and down
to the conference room. A dark-wood rectangular table stood
in the middle with twelve black leather office chairs around it.
The yellow carpet had crease marks from a recent vacuum-
ing.

Finley led Monroe and me to a door with a key lock at the
back of the room. It opened into a stairway with a single flight
of stairs down to the floor under The Spa Club. On the wall just
inside the door, a ladder rose to a trapdoor and, I figured, the
roof. The ladder and the trapdoor looked original to the building. The stairs down looked like an afterthought, added when
The Spa Club or an earlier tenant needed extra space.

We went down the stairs to another hall. Three open doors
lined the left side of the hall, and at the end there was a heavy
exit door. Finley walked us past the first open door. Unused furniture, a couple of mattresses, and an unplugged refrigerator

crowded the room. The second door opened into a windowless space, empty except for an office chair. Finley and Raj pushed Monroe inside. Raj closed the door and locked it.

The third room was a twin of the second.

"In," Finley said.

I stepped toward the door like there was no place I would rather go, then spun and lifted my knee into Finley's gut. He made a sound like air blowing from a narrow-necked bag and fell to the floor. The door at the end of the hall was three or four steps away. If it was unlocked, I could be through it before Raj and the others realized what was happening. I spun toward it.

Then my feet were no longer on the floor. Someone had kicked them out from under me. As I fell, I looked and saw Raj. He'd knocked me down.

Finley was lying on the hallway floor, doubled over, moaning and swearing. I looked at him eye to eye.

Raj pulled me into the room and set me down next to the chair. As he stepped back into the hall, he faced me so only I could see him. He mouthed a word or two but I couldn't read him.

Then the door slammed and a key turned in the lock.

I stayed on the floor for awhile, staring at the ceiling. The paint looked new but a thin line marked an old crack that was starting to show through. I traced the crack from one wall across the ceiling to another, then traced it back. The gray carpet was soft enough. Still, I stood up and looked around the room. There was nothing to see except the chair, metal legged with a vinyl seat cushion. And the walls, the cracked ceiling, and the carpeted floor. And the locked door.

The chair in the middle of the room was strange. Why had

they bothered to put it in the room and another one like it in the next room? I kicked the chair leg. It was solid. Someone could be tied to a chair like that, I decided. And then someone else could hurt the person tied to the chair. Or maybe they put the chairs in the rooms so that we wouldn't have to sit on the floor. Maybe they were being hospitable.

I liked that idea better. I sat on the chair.

I put my hands around the chair back to see how it would feel. Scary. I stood and went to the door. I looked at my watch. It said 5:41.

In less than an hour and a half, Lucinda would climb through the stairwell to The Spa Club. Maybe in less time than that, Johnson's crew would come back and tie me to the chair.

I pulled my cell phone from my pocket and dialed Lucinda's number.

Before it rang, a key sounded in the door lock and I hung up.

Finley stepped in, gun drawn. His face was a shade too pale and he bent like his belly was tender where I'd kneed him. He looked like he wanted to shoot me. He said, "Your phone."

I handed it to him.

"Thank you," he said and turned to the door.

"Sorry about the stomach," I said.

He said nothing to that. He went out and locked the door behind him.

I paced the room. Five steps long, four steps wide. Six steps from corner to corner. I put in a mile or two, back and forth and around.

Then I went to the wall that I shared with the room where Finley had put Monroe. I put my ear to the wall.

Silence.

I knocked on the wall.

More silence.

I called softly, "Hey!" Anyone standing near the door to the room would hear me but I called anyway. "Monroe!"

After a few seconds, Monroe's voice answered through the wall, "What?"

"If you're locked in a room in this building with just a chair, how do you get out?" I said.

"Is this a fucking riddle?"

"You know this building better than I do. How do you get out?"

"You don't, you stupid fuck."

"I'm getting out," I said.

He said nothing to that.

"Monroe?" I called.

Silence.

I went back to pacing.

When I got tired of pacing, I sat in the chair.

When I got tired of sitting in the chair, I stood, picked up the chair, swung it as hard as I could, and released it. It flew across the room and hit the wall by the door. Two of the chair legs punched through the drywall.

A moment later, a key unlocked the door and Finley stepped inside again. He still held the gun. Color had mostly returned to his face and he was standing straighter than before. He looked at me. He looked at the chair sticking out of the wall. He went to the chair and yanked it. Pieces of drywall fell to the carpet and the chair came free. One of the legs had poked through the outside wall and light shined through from the hallway.

Finley shook his head like he was disgusted with me, carried the chair out of the room, and locked the door.

I paced some more, then stretched out on the floor and

looked at the crack on the ceiling. If Finley would give me sandpaper, some brushes, and a can of paint, I could fix it.

I closed my eyes, opened them again.

The crack still reached across the ceiling. I was still locked in the room.

I stayed like that for a long time. It felt like days and weeks. I sometimes looked at my watch. It said 5:58. Then it said 6:10. Later it said 6:40.

That meant Lucinda was probably in the building, climbing the stairs.

Then my watch said 6:50. That meant Johnson and his crew probably had Lucinda in their hands or would soon. There wasn't a thing I could do to help her.

At 6:55 a key rattled in the lock.

I stood and moved to the door, ready to fight my way out—to do anything I needed to do to get to Lucinda.

The door swung open.

Finley wasn't there with his gun. The gang leader Rafael stood in the doorway. He grinned and said, "*Hola.*"

I looked at him, confused. "What are you—?"

He stepped into the room. "*He* called," he said, sticking a thumb over his shoulder.

Raj stepped in behind him.

I shook my head, confused. "What are you doing?"

He looked nervous. "Trying to save your ass—and my own."

"Are you with Monroe, or Johnson and Finley?"

"I'm with myself," he said and stepped back into the hall. Rafael and I followed.

"I don't understand," I said.

Raj looked down the hall toward the stairs to The Spa Club. "There's not time."

"I'm not going anywhere," I said.

He looked furious. "Don't be an asshole. Finley told me he'd figured out Monroe was making a power play and told me to come along when he nailed him. If I hadn't, he'd have locked me up with you. He'll be right back—you've got to get out of here."

I shook my head. "I need to check the stairwell. My partner's supposed to be there."

"It's too late. You've got to leave."

"Not without Lucinda."

"Jesus! I'll check for her myself," he said and yelled at Rafael, "Get him the hell out of here."

That would need to be good enough. Rafael and I headed for the exit door.

As we reached it, a voice came from the other end of the hall. "Hey!"

It was Finley. He held his pistol so he could shoot us in the back.

"Keep going," Raj yelled at me and Rafael. He stepped toward Finley. "It's all right, Peter—"

"Stop!" Finley yelled.

Rafael and I kept going.

Finley fired his gun. A deafening blast filled the hall and a bullet slammed into the steel plating on the exit door. I reached for the door handle, pushed, and looked over my shoulder. In the hazy light, Raj was running toward Finley. He ran the way people run toward a bad accident. Not that they can do anything to stop what already has happened or the blood that will pour. Not that they really know why they're running. Finley watched him come, his pistol level, his lips tight, his jaw square.

Finley shot again. The blast ripped through the hallway.

Raj flew backward. He landed on his back, his eyes wide, his chest bloody.

Rafael shoved me through the door.

I tried to stop. "Get Raj!"

Rafael kept pushing. "He's dead!"

Raj was dead. Of course he was. You don't take a bullet in the chest from a .40-caliber Glock and live. You don't stare at a hallway ceiling with wide unblinking eyes if you're still feeling pain.

"Shit!" I yelled. Another shot from Finley's gun slammed into the closing door.

We were in a gray lobby by a service elevator. Two Mexican kids held the elevator door open. They were sixteen or seventeen years old, wearing black T-shirts and low-rider jeans. One of them had on a black baseball cap with a silver star on it. He grinned at Rafael and me with a gold-capped front tooth. "What's up?" he said, like we were meeting on a street corner.

The kids moved aside to let us into the elevator and one punched the button for the ground floor. Finley burst into the lobby as the elevator doors closed.

TWENTY-SIX

WHEN THE ELEVATOR DOORS opened again, Rafael's friends stepped out, looked left and right, and signaled for us to follow. We ran across the lobby and out the front door. A gray BMW sedan and a jacked-up Chevy Silverado pickup stood at the curb, engines running.

Rafael's friends climbed into the pickup.

Rafael knocked fists with the valet. "*Gracias*," he said.

"Far as I know, you're not here," the doorman said. "I didn't see you coming and I don't see you going."

"'Course you don't," said Rafael, and he slipped a roll of bills into the doorman's hand.

I said nothing. Pointing out the video camera that fed everything we were doing to the Spa Club monitor room seemed like bad manners.

We got into the BMW and the doorman waved at me. "Have a good night, Mr. Kozmarski—and drive safely."

The kid at the wheel of the pickup punched the accelerator. The tires spun and screeched and the truck leapt forward. It shot down the driveway, tilted onto the street, and disappeared to the south.

"Fucking clowns," Rafael said. He shifted into Drive and we rode down the driveway and pulled into the street.

We went south to Oak Street, across to Lake Shore Drive, and south again. The evening traffic had thinned and Rafael weaved steadily around slower cars. To the east, a green light glowed on a breakwater wall a quarter mile off the beach. After the green light, there was nothing but darkness.

"Where are we going?" I said.

"My part of town. Johnson can't get you there."

I considered that. "Thanks, but I'll do it alone. You can drop me downtown."

"You got a car?" he said.

"No," I admitted.

"A gun?"

"No."

"Cops are looking for you at your office and your house. Johnson's crew is definitely hunting for you. What're you going to do with no car, no gun, and no place to sleep?"

I thought about that for awhile. "Fine," I said. "Let's go to your part of town."

He glanced in the rearview mirror. "Right," he said. Then he stepped on the accelerator.

"What's the rush?"

He tipped his chin toward the backseat. "Like I said—look behind us."

I did. A white SUV sped after us, changing lanes when we did, closing the gap. Through the glare and shadow of its front window I saw two men. The one in the passenger seat looked like Finley. I wasn't sure about the driver. He could've been the guy who took my pistol from me in Monroe's office.

"Can this thing go any faster?" I said.

Rafael laughed and sped up. We shot toward the downtown lights, the SUV behind us. The tall, black-windowed apartments in Lake Point Tower loomed on the left. On the other side, our headlights flashed on a big American flag tied to the side of a construction crane. It rose in the air on the cold breeze and fell like a giant hand waving good-bye.

"How did you get into The Spa Club?" I said.

Rafael checked the rearview mirror again and said, "Raj called. He said you were in trouble. Said it was getting too deep and he wanted out. Said if I didn't come get you, Johnson might decide to make you go away for good. You know, any time I can fuck up Johnson's plans I'm going to do it. Anyway, Raj is an okay guy—or was. That was ugly, what that man did to him."

"Peter Finley."

"Whoever. I mean, with friends like him—"

I glanced at Rafael. The light from outside glinted in his eyes. None of the tattooed words on his bicep said *KILL* but the inked blades and guns meant it just the same. "What do you know about friends?" I said.

He checked the mirror, then looked at me. "What? I came and got you and I don't hardly know your ass. I didn't see your other friends coming for you."

No, I'd left a friend behind. If Lucinda had managed to get to the fourteenth-floor stairwell, they had her now and I was riding away from her at eighty miles an hour. "Do you have a cell phone?" I said.

He looked at me like I was a caveman. "I got three. You need one?"

I said I did. He handed me a phone and I punched Lucinda's number into it.

It rang three times and a man's voice answered—Johnson's.

"Let me talk to Lucinda, Earl," I said.

He yelled into the phone, "Get back here—"

I hung up on him.

Rafael glared at me and said, "Gimme." I put the phone in his hand, and he rolled down his window and chucked it out. "You gave my phone number to Earl Johnson," he said and shook his head.

We crossed the river, went around a bend, and flew along the harbor. In front of us, a stoplight turned yellow, then red. Rafael hit the accelerator and we went into the intersection. I looked over my shoulder. The SUV followed us through, missing a crossing car by inches.

"*Muy loco*," Rafael said like he admired the driver. He pulled out a second cell phone, tapped the keypad, and talked to someone in Spanish. He added in English, or mostly, "*Sí*, Eighteenth and Throop Street," then laughed and hung up.

I kept my eyes on the SUV. Finley leaned out of the passenger window. He had a weapon in his hand. He leveled it so it pointed at the back window of Rafael's BMW.

"Do you have a gun?" I said.

Rafael sounded annoyed. "You think I would bring a weapon to a club owned by cops? You got to be kidding."

Finley shot, and the bullet thunked into metal behind us.

"Under the seat!" Rafael said.

I reached under the seat and pulled out a sawed-off Remington shotgun. Single shot.

"Loaded?" I said.

He nodded. "But only one shell."

I looked at him like he must be kidding. He wasn't. "What kind of thug are you with only one round?"

"A thug who's got one more round than you, right?" he said.

I unrolled my window and leaned out, pointed the shotgun at Finley.

He didn't know I had only one shot. He disappeared into the SUV.

I slid into the BMW.

The next stoplight was green. We flew through the intersection and along Grant Park.

Finley's hand, holding his pistol, jutted out of the SUV window again. He fired the gun, missed, and fired again.

"Shoot the asshole!" Rafael said.

I leaned out the window again, aimed the shotgun at Finley.

He squeezed off another two shots.

I waited for the pain that would seep into me if he hit me. None came.

I looked down the sawed-off barrel until its tip lined up with Finley's head.

"Shoot him!" Rafael yelled.

I couldn't pull the trigger. I'd already shot one cop too many. Another cop—even Finley, who was gunning for me—was too much.

I lowered the gun a few inches, aimed at the front tire. If I blew it out, the SUV would stop and we would leave Finley behind. That seemed better than killing him.

I pulled the trigger.

The kick of the shotgun threw me back but I kept my eyes on the SUV. The right headlight went dark. The white paint on the front hood was flecked with black. But the SUV kept coming. The tire was still good.

I slipped into the car again, and Rafael looked in the rearview mirror. He made a sound that was half laugh and half howl. "You missed! You have a fucking shotgun! How can you miss?"

I had nothing to say so I said nothing.

"Jesus!" he said. "You don't get no second chances." He accelerated through the next intersection, glanced in the mirror, and added, "They're coming."

I looked. The SUV had closed to three car lengths. Finley's arm stuck out of the window with his gun.

"Pretend to shoot again," Rafael said.

It seemed like as good an idea as anything else, so I turned and stuck the shotgun out the window. Finley's arm disappeared and the SUV dropped back a couple of car lengths.

"Here goes—" Rafael said, and, before I could ask, he whipped into the turn lane at Roosevelt Road and slid around the corner.

The SUV came after us, went wide, almost ended up on the concrete median, but corrected and slid in behind. Finley's arm came out with the gun.

"Go!" I yelled.

The BMW shot forward, the SUV right behind, Finley's hand steadying toward our back window.

I leaned out the window with the shotgun.

But Finley didn't buy it. He stuck his head out too. He leveled his gun. He pointed the barrel at me. His face was serious. He took no pleasure in what he was about to do.

Then Rafael said, "Ahhh." He said it the way you do for a doctor. Again I had no time to ask. The wheels of the BMW hit a lip in the road, the kind that would give the car a light jolt if we'd been moving at half the speed. The BMW lifted as high as the shocks would take it and came down again.

The SUV hit the lip too. I watched as Finley bounced against the SUV door frame. I watched as he dropped the gun. It bounced crazily on the pavement, glanced off the side of a delivery truck, and skidded across the concrete. Finley watched it too. He yelled something that I couldn't make out. Then he pulled himself back into the car.

I slid inside and grinned at Rafael.

"What happened?"

"We just got a second chance."

We flew west on Roosevelt, over the South Branch of the river, over a railroad yard, over the Dan Ryan Expressway. Twice, stoplights turned red and Rafael pulled into the oncoming lanes, hit the horn, and forced his way through. Twice, the SUV followed us.

We zigged to the south on Halsted and, a mile later, zagged to the west. We drove into Pilsen, the closest thing to a Mexico City neighborhood north of the Rio Grande. The yellow and red business signs were Spanish, no translation. We sped past the Tortilleria Del Rey bakery, past La Chamba—a storefront that doubled as a union office and a temporary worker business— and past the Casa Castañeda appliance store. Painted on the brick storefronts between the signs, murals showed the Virgin Mary, a leather jacketed ranchero, a mariachi player holding an accordion with a haloed picture of Jesus looking over him, women dancing, a hairy human skull in a blue baseball cap. Music poured from the open door of a *tienda*. We were in Rafael's part of town.

"Now what?" I said.

Rafael pulled out his cell phone. "Now we send these guys home," he said.

He tapped the phone keypad. When someone answered, he said, "Okay?"

The person he was talking to must have said yes.

We flew past South Throop Street. "Here we go," Rafael said.

Ahead of us, a burgundy sedan nosed into the street from an alley between a real estate firm with a blue awning and an accountant's office called La Oficina.

When we were about forty feet from the alley, Rafael said, "Now!"

The sedan rolled from the alley into the middle of the street. Half a dozen guys were pushing it. No one was in the driver's seat.

We swerved around the sedan, just missing an oncoming delivery truck.

Finley's SUV didn't swerve. There was no time. There was no place to go.

It buried its front end in the side of the sedan.

Rafael took his foot off the accelerator and checked the rear-view mirror. The Sedan horn, shorted by the crash, blew mournfully.

Rafael shook his head. "Fucking clowns," he said.

We drove another quarter mile, turned left onto Ashland, and turned again on 19th Street. The town houses were two and three stories high, maybe eighty years old, fronted with brick or vinyl siding and concrete steps to sit on in the warm months, built so close together that the roofs almost touched. We rode a half block in, and Rafael pulled to the curb and cut the engine.

He sighed and stretched his arms toward the car roof. "We're home," he said.

I looked out the window at a two-story yellow brick town house. "Yours?"

"Hell, no. Yours for now."

We got out and Rafael walked to the back of the car. He rubbed a finger on the hole that Finley had shot into the trunk. He shook his head. "Now that pisses me off," he said.

I looked up and down the street. Three lots away from the yellow two-story, a church was squeezed between houses. Its brown brick walls rose above the surrounding roofs. The side wall that faced us had a mural, lit by a spotlight mounted on the roof of the neighboring house. The mural showed a naked woman standing in a canoe. A man stood on the water next to the canoe. Four red roses surrounded the man and the woman and the canoe.

"What's that mean?" I said.

Rafael glanced at the mural and started up the path to the yellow house. "Hell if I know. What's anything mean?"

TWENTY-SEVEN

A SMALL, HEAVY WOMAN with a long black braid opened the door. I put her in her early thirties, though she could've been younger. She flashed a nervous smile at Rafael and stared at me with dark suspicious eyes.

Rafael talked with her in Spanish and she opened the door and said, "Come."

We stepped inside.

"This is Sanchia," Rafael said. "She'll take care of you."

I reached my hand to shake hers. "I'm Joe."

She left my hand hanging in the air. "I know."

The light in the front hall was dim. A Spanish-language video with a laugh track played on the television in the living room. A boy who looked about seven was stretched on the floor watching. Another boy, a couple of years older, was on a couch. The house smelled of cooking—low-simmering meat and sweet-sour vegetables, smells I knew from Mom's house if you added spice.

"Come on," Rafael said and he led me down the hall into the kitchen.

We sat at the kitchen table and Sanchia spooned rice from a pot and ladled pieces of pork shoulder and tomatillos into bowls. A picture of the Virgin Mary watched from above the stove. Sanchia put the bowls in front of us and got us two beers from the refrigerator. After she warmed some tortillas for us, she left the room.

"Who is she?" I said.

Rafael looked like he was deciding how much to tell me. "My brother's wife," he said.

"Yeah? Where's your brother?"

"In jail. Johnson put him there. I'm taking care of Sanchia right now."

I took a bite of pork and rice. It warmed me like nothing else had in weeks, maybe months. "Seems like she's taking care of you too."

He lifted his beer bottle and toasted it against an imaginary bottle. "Family," he said.

I lifted my bottle, the same. "Can't live without them."

We ate then without talking, like we hadn't eaten in days and wouldn't eat again for a week. Sanchia came in again twice, refilled our bowls, and gave us more beer.

When I was full, I watched as Rafael helped himself to a fourth bowl. When he finished, he wiped his chin and looked me in the eyes, aware that I'd been watching him. "What?" he said.

"You didn't rescue me and bring me here for dinner because you're my friend. What do you get for helping me out?"

Rafael looked insulted, but not very. "It is a favor. Friends do favors."

"Uh-huh. What kind of favor do you want from me in return?"

He shrugged. "First, let's see if we keep you alive. If we do, we can talk about favors later."

"You know, I've got a bad record of filling obligations."

He smiled big. "That don't surprise me. Anyway, you already give me something. You help me fuck with Earl Johnson."

He stood and went into the hall, came back a minute later with a bag. He pulled out a thin black disposable cell phone and gave it to me. "If you need to call me, use this. Don't use Sanchia's phone. We keep her clean—she's got enough trouble already."

I took the phone. "You keep extras lying around?"

"Sure. You never know when you need one."

"Thanks," I said.

"You got four hours of talk time. Throw it out when you're done."

I said I would.

"Now stand up," he said.

"Why?"

"Just stand the fuck up," he said.

I did.

He looked me up and down, measuring me. "I'll bring you clothes in the morning."

"Thanks," I said again.

"Give me the phone." I gave it to him and he punched in his own number. "Day or night, you call me if there's trouble."

"You're a saint," I said.

He smiled again. "I'll shoot anyone who doesn't say so." He walked back into the hall, saying, "Be a good boy tonight."

A minute later, the front door opened and closed, and I was alone with Rafael's sister-in-law and her two boys. The Virgin Mary watched me from above the stove. A wooden kitchen clock, shaped like a horse, ticked loudly. Up the hall, the television laugh track heard something hysterical.

I thought about slipping out the back door into the cold night. I could call a cab on the phone Rafael gave me, and it would take me anywhere I wanted to go. But I didn't know where that would be. Lucinda needed rescuing but going back to The Spa Club alone and without a gun seemed like a bad idea. Going to Corrine's house or Mom's would bring my trouble to them.

I dialed Bill Gubman's home phone number. His wife picked up.

"Hi, Eileen," I said.

She recognized my voice. "Joe—" She said. She didn't need to say anything else to let me know she'd heard about my problems and whatever else the TV news had made up about me.

"Is Bill there?"

"No," she said. "He's working late—"

"Thanks, Eileen. I'll try him at the station."

"Joe?"

"Yeah?" I said, bracing myself for another friend telling me I should turn myself in.

"Take care of yourself," she said.

"Thanks," I said and hung up.

I called the department and asked to talk to Bill. The desk operator said he was out of his office. "It's important that I talk to him. Can you give me a number where I can reach him?"

"I'm sorry," she said. She didn't sound sorry.

"Put me through to his voice mail?"

She did.

I left a frantic message. "Johnson has Lucinda at The Spa Club," I said. "I don't know what they're going to do with her but it won't be good. It's time to end this. You need to break up Johnson's crew now, you understand?" I left the number of the disposable cell phone and said, "Call me as soon as you get this."

He didn't call. I sat alone for an hour, and the phone never rang.

I fished the FBI card that Stuart Felicano had given me from my wallet. He'd asked me to call if I had any information. I'd told myself I never would, but I'd slipped the card into my wallet anyway. Now I wondered if that meant I'd always known I was a liar.

I dialed the cell number printed on the card.

After three rings, Felicano picked up.

"It's Joe Kozmarski," I said.

If I'd said I was a large roach, he might've sounded happier to talk with me. "What do you want?" he said.

"I've got information," I said. "If you want Johnson and his crew, I can tell you where to find them tonight. You can get them on about thirty charges. Prostitution. Grand theft. Racketeering. Kidnapping too. I'll testify for you. You don't have to promise me anything."

There was a long pause. Then he said, "You're too late. We're off the case."

"What do you mean?" I almost dropped the phone.

"I mean, your friend Bill Gubman talked to my boss, and

my boss talked to me. It's part of a new spirit of cooperation between city and federal agencies, she said. This is a city matter. We're letting the city cops handle it."

"But Johnson has my partner—"

"Tell it to Gubman."

"I tried but I can't reach him."

"Sorry," he said.

"Sorry?" I shouted.

"Not even very," he said.

I hung up.

I paced the kitchen for awhile. That didn't help, so I walked to the living room and sat on a chair next to the boy on the floor and the one on the couch. Their mother was somewhere else, probably upstairs. The video was ending, the credits rolling up the screen, and it all washed over me like a haze.

The seven-year-old rolled onto his back and stared at me. He looked worried and I figured I did too.

So I tried to smile. "Hey," I said.

He smiled. "Hey."

"What's your name?"

"Emilio."

His mother swept downstairs and into the room. She said, "*¡Emilio, vete a tu cuarto!*"—*Go to your room.* The boy got up and shuffled toward the hall. Sanchia turned to the older boy. "*Tu tambien.*" He got up and followed his brother.

"*Buenas noches,*" I said.

The seven-year-old giggled.

His mother didn't. She turned to me. "You will wait here. My younger son will sleep in his brother's room. You can sleep in his bed."

"That's all right," I said. "I can sleep down here."

"No," she said and gave me a look that let me know I was in her house and I would do as she told me.

"Thank you," I said.

She nodded once and followed her boys upstairs.

A bath turned on. Sanchia talked with her boys in Spanish and English. I sat and listened and tried not to think.

When the house got quiet, I went up the stairs. A light was on in a bedroom—the younger boy's. Toy cars, a tower made of Tinkertoys, and about a dozen jigsaw puzzles of jungle scenes and birds, neatly constructed and lined up edge to edge, covered the floor. The bed was unmade, the covers pushed to the bottom. Crayon pictures of birds hung on the walls. I went in and closed the door, stepped through the mess to the window, and opened the shade. Across a gap of about four feet, another window and another shade faced the house from next door. If you leaned out far enough, you could kiss your neighbor.

I closed the shade, sat on the bed, and took off my shoes, socks, and pants. I straightened the sheets. They smelled like soap and the gentle sweat of a kid. I climbed in and turned off the lamp, then closed my eyes and breathed deep.

After awhile, I slept, and sometime during the night I dreamed a good dream, one that I'd dreamed before. I was with Corrine and Jason. We were on a powerboat, motoring across blue-green Caribbean water. The sky was clear and the sun gleamed on the ocean ripples. We wore swimsuits and cotton shirts that billowed in the salt breeze. We said nothing to each other. We didn't need to say anything. We were happy. Happy.

A hand shook my shoulder. I opened my eyes, expecting to see Corrine and Jason. The room was dark. The hand shook my shoulder some more. "Wake up!" whispered a voice, a woman's, accented Spanish—Sanchia's voice, I realized when she whispered again, "Wake up!"

"What?" I managed to say.

"Get up!" she whispered. "You must go."

Other voices were yelling somewhere else. Downstairs. Outside. Men's voices.

"Who—?" And then I knew and I sat bolt upright in bed.

"Quick," Sanchia said and she stepped out of the bedroom.

I put on my pants and shoes and followed her into the dimly lighted hall.

The men outside were quiet now.

Sanchia opened a hall closet and took out an aluminum stepladder. She set it under a ceiling trapdoor.

"That go to the roof?" I asked.

She nodded and pointed toward the side of the house. "Three houses and you go inside. They wait for you," she said.

Men shouted outside the house again.

I climbed the ladder, unfastened a latch, opened the heavy door, and heaved myself onto a flat tar roof.

Downstairs, someone kicked the front door, kicked it again, and kicked it a third time. Wood splintered and the door slammed open.

I turned and said, "Thanks," but Sanchia was already putting the ladder back in the closet.

Heavy footsteps ran up the stairs.

I lowered the trapdoor and heard the latch snap shut, then stood still and silent in the cold night.

A man's voice yelled at Sanchia. Not Finley's. The voice of one of the other men in Johnson's crew. He wanted to know where I was.

I didn't hear Sanchia's answer.

He yelled louder.

She yelled back, "*¡No comprendo!*"

The night was black and a cold breeze cut through my clothes. What could I do? Sanchia had said, *Three houses and you go inside*.

I looked both ways. On one side, there were two roofs and then the church with the mural of the naked woman in a canoe. On the other side, there were just roofs, four or five feet apart on the closely built houses.

They wait for you, Sanchia had said.

I inched quietly to the edge of the roof. In the shadows twenty feet down, garbage cans stood on the path between the houses. They would break my fall but not much.

I estimated the distance between Sanchia's roof and the next one, breathed deep, and jumped. My foot caught the edge of the roof and I fell forward. Anyone under me would've thought an ox fell on the house. I got up, ran across the roof, and jumped again, landing on my feet.

Three houses.

The next gap was wider than the first two but I didn't slow. I cleared it with plenty to spare.

In the middle of the roof, there was a trapdoor that matched the one on Sanchia's house.

I ran to it and reached to open it but it opened as if on its own and a hand came out and then a man's cheerful round face. "*¡Hola!*" the man said. "Come in before you freeze."

I went down a stepladder into a dark house. "Come with me," the man said and he led me to the stairway and down-stairs. In the living room, he gestured at a sofa. "You can sleep here. I'll get some blankets." As he went to get them, he whistled cheerfully. It was three in the morning, a stranger had dropped through his ceiling into his house, and he was whistling.

I sat on the sofa and he brought two folded blankets and set them next to me. "Sleep now," he said. "You're safe here." And, whistling, he climbed the stairs to the second floor.

TWENTY-EIGHT

THE MAN DIDN'T TELL me his name and I didn't ask for it. He left me with two blankets and a place to sleep, surrounded by strange sounds and smells, and I was eight miles from home and could have been on the other side of the world. I stretched out under the blankets with my shoes on.

When I closed my eyes, fear surged through me as if another hand would shake me awake and tell me to run. So I opened my eyes and stared at the dark ceiling and at a glint that bounced off the glass front of a china cabinet, or maybe it was a mirror—it was too dark to tell and I didn't get up to find out. I twisted David Russo's wedding ring on my finger. I counted the minutes and hours and every one of them was as dark as the last, until the first sunlight filtered into the room a little after six. I could see that the glass with the glint in it was a mirror and then I closed my eyes and slept.

I slept hard and dull, and when I woke a little after eleven, I stayed on the couch and wished I still was sleeping. The man with the round, cheerful face was in the kitchen talking with someone in Spanish—Rafael, I realized. Then a cell phone rang and Rafael answered it in English and talked some more. I tried not to listen. I stared at the ceiling and wondered if I could ever get to the place where I'd been during the good dream I was having before Sanchia shook my shoulder, a happy place with Corrine and Jason.

After awhile, the doorbell rang and Rafael went to it through the living room. He saw I was awake, nodded at me, and said, "*Buenos*."

I nodded back.

He stepped outside to the front porch and talked for awhile, then came in again and sat on the side of the couch like a father waking up his kid. "Hey," he said, "you got a visitor."

For a moment that made me glad. I figured Johnson had freed Lucinda and she'd come to see me. Maybe there was no sense in it but I sat up expecting to see her.

Bob Monroe stood inside the front door. He wore the same brown tracksuit he'd had on when Finley had broken up our talk about bringing down Johnson. He looked like he hadn't slept and his left eye was bloodshot.

"Morning," he said. The confidence he usually had in his voice was gone.

I stated the obvious. "You got out."

"I guess so."

"Lucinda?"

"Your partner?" He shook his head like he was embarrassed. "They've still got her."

"Why?" I said as if it was his fault.

He shrugged.

"How did you escape?"

Another shrug. "They let me go. After Finley got back from

chasing you—limping and one arm in a sling—he saw the receipts on my desk and worked it out. They unlocked my door around nine this morning. Johnson's saying he didn't rip us off. He's saying he's played it straight. But they've got him locked in the room where you were. No chair, though."

"What happened to Lucinda?"

"They say she caused a lot of trouble last night—scared the hell out of a seventy-year-old alderman who came out of a room while a couple of the guys were taking her from the stairwell. What were you thinking, telling her to come to the club?"

Now *I* shrugged. "I thought I could use a hand if someone locked me in a room with only a chair."

"Seems to me you did all right without her."

"Where is she now? Is she all right?"

He nodded. "She's in the room next to Johnson."

"Why?" I asked again.

This time he told me. "Finley's still not totally convinced Johnson's the enemy. Same with some of the others. They let me out so I could find you and bring you back. They want us to explain the evidence. They want Johnson to defend himself."

"They're holding a trial?"

"Something like that. They think keeping your partner will get you to come back."

"Why do they want me so bad?"

"You gave me the bank receipts. Why wouldn't they want you?"

He had a point, and, even if he didn't, I needed to go back for Lucinda. But I would have liked to go back with Bill Gubman beside me and a SWAT team in front of us.

"Okay," I said and I got up.

Rafael handed me a bag with the clothes he'd promised—a

new pair of jeans, a new white sweatshirt, and a used brown leather jacket. While I cleaned up and changed into them, the round-faced man cooked us a meal of scrambled eggs and chorizo. When I came into the kitchen, Rafael and Monroe were sitting at the kitchen table and the man stood at the stove, whistling again like there was nothing he liked more than serving breakfast to cop killers, gangbangers, and thieves.

After we ate, Monroe and I drove back to The Spa Club in Monroe's car. Outside, the sun was shining, the sky clear, the wind calm for the first time in a week. I felt like we were driving toward our deaths. I glanced at Monroe. He was watching the road, lips pursed, unhappy. Maybe he felt like we were driving to our deaths too.

I said, "What about Raj?"

The question shook Monroe out of his thoughts. "What about him?"

"Finley shot him."

He shook his head. "No, he didn't—not as far as you're concerned. There's a newspaper in the backseat. Take a look at it."

I reached into the backseat, picked up a copy of the *Sun-Times*. The front-page headline said COP GUNNED DOWN IN ROBBERY. The story explained that neighbors found Raj's body on the sidewalk outside his house after hearing gunshots. His wallet was gone. The police had no suspects, though one of the neighbors reported having seen a black male, approximately six foot two and a hundred ninety pounds, acting suspiciously an hour before the shooting.

Monroe said, "We'll support Raj's wife, and his kids will grow up knowing their dad was a good cop."

"Finley gets away with it?"

Monroe shook his head some more. "Now's not the time. Finley's not sure whose side he's on. He sees the banking evidence. He knows Johnson screwed him. But they've been buddies for a long time. If we want him on our side, we've got to be forgiving."

"I'm not ready to forgive."

"We'll see," he said, though I didn't know what there was to see.

At The Spa Club, Monroe pulled through the circular driveway, passed the valet, and parked in a fire lane on the side of the building. We got out and he pocketed the keys. He said, "I want to be able to get to my car—just in case."

I nodded. "I hope you don't mind giving me and Lucinda a lift—just in case."

"It'll be my pleasure."

We rode the elevator to the fourteenth floor.

When the door opened, the lounge was empty. No one sat at the tables. No one tended bar. No one stood at the hostess station.

"First time we've closed in seven months," Monroe said.

As we stepped out, two of Johnson's crew came from the hall behind the hostess desk. Someone must've been watching the elevator from the video monitor room.

One of them gave Monroe an almost friendly smile. "Hey, Bob."

Monroe raised his hands so the men could frisk him, and I followed his lead. Then the men steered us down the hall and into the conference room.

Finley sat at the head of the table, his left arm in a cast, a bruise above his left eye. The man to his left had a bandage on his chin. I figured he was the driver when the SUV crashed into the car that Rafael's friends rolled into the street. The other members of Johnson's crew sat around the table. Lucinda sat between two of them. I looked her up and down. She was wearing a long-sleeved black T-shirt with a V front that hinted at the skin of her breasts. She had a bruise on her jaw and I wondered if she'd picked it up while fighting Johnson's crew when they pulled her out of the stairwell, or if they'd come into her room and given it to her later. She locked eyes with me, no expression on her face, no fear. I couldn't read her thoughts.

Monroe and I took two chairs across the table from her.

Finley picked up a phone, punched a few keys, and said, "We're ready." He did this once more, and a minute later the guy who'd been manning the video monitors came in. Then the door in the back opened and two more men accompanied Johnson into the conference room. Johnson sat in the one remaining chair and the two men stood behind him.

Johnson looked around the table like he was measuring each person. When his eyes rested on me, his lips curled into a slightly amused smile.

TWENTY-NINE

FINLEY LEANED BACK, LOOKED at Lucinda, then me and Monroe, and said, "Okay, Bob, tell us what you've got."

Monroe said, "Do you have the reports and bank receipts?"

Finley reached down to the carpet and brought up a leather case. He took out a stack of stapled packets. "Copies for everyone." He passed the packets around the table.

I figured everyone had seen what was in them already but Monroe waited until the shuffling of pages stopped. He said, "Two days ago, Joe brought me some bank receipts. He got them before he joined us, when he was investigating us for a group of clients that included the developers of Southshore Village. The receipts worried me," he said and looked at Johnson. "They *angered* me. Earl handpicked most of us, me included. And when we agreed to join him, we had a clear understanding. We'd work together. No freelancing. No cutting each other out of a good thing." He looked from face to face at the rest of the crew. "We've all been cops long enough to know that's what the stupid guys do, the ones we catch after one or two robberies because they turn on each other and fuck each other up."

Some of the other guys nodded.

Monroe looked at Johnson again. "But that's what he's been doing. He's been fucking us up, every one of us. So I did a little digging. I got the reports for the robberies we didn't do but that looked like what we were doing. As you can see, the dates match the receipts."

The guys in the crew paged through the packets and murmured. Except Johnson. He sat stone-faced and silent.

Monroe moved in for the kill. "I also remember what Earl told me when he asked me to join him. He said he'd stand by me no matter how bad the heat got, unless I crossed him by going solo and pocketing money for myself. If I did that, he said there'd be no forgiveness. I didn't have to ask him what he meant. I understood. I'm guessing he said the same thing to each one of us here, and I'm guessing you understood too."

More guys nodded.

Finley turned to me. "How did you get the bank receipts?"

Part of me wanted to admit that Bill Gubman had fabricated the receipts and handed the stack of them to me. I felt like the building would fall down under us if I told the truth and maybe that would be good. I said, "A woman who hired me to locate her missing son has access to credit, banking, and mortgage records. Her son was dead when I found him but she was grateful anyway. I call her from time to time when I need information."

"What's her name and where does she work?" Finley said.

I shook my head. "Sorry."

He looked angry but spoke calmly. "I didn't ask if you *want* to tell me. I asked what her name is."

Again I shook my head. "When Southshore Corporation hired me, I started off by staking out the construction sites I figured you would hit. I always got it wrong. If I went to a place on the Northside, you would hit the Westside. If I went to the Westside, you would hit downtown. But one night I got lucky. I was half asleep outside a depot near the airport when a white van pulled up and a man got out and cut the lock off the gate. He was alone, and, when he turned to get back into the van and drive inside, I couldn't believe what I saw. The man was Earl Johnson, and I'd known Earl since we went through the academy together." Like a shark that keeps swimming, I figured if I kept talking I would stay alive. I said, "After that night, my job got easy. Instead of staking out construction sites and hoping to get lucky, I just followed Earl. Sometimes he went out with the crew, and sometimes he went out alone. I figured he was ripping off the rest of you guys. But that wasn't my worry. Not then. Not yet."

The room was quiet. Then Finley asked again, "What's the name of the woman who gave you the receipts?"

I showed him my palms. "Sorry."

He nodded to the two men who were guarding Johnson. One of them walked around the table and came up behind me.

I braced for what would come next.

"She's my aunt," Lucinda said. "Her name is Marta Navarro and she works for a credit company. I sent her to Joe when my cousin disappeared. I can give you her number."

"What is it?" he said.

"It's in my cell phone—which you took away from me."

The man behind me said, "Want me to get it?"

"Later," Finley said. He nodded at Lucinda and asked me, "How does your partner fit in?"

"She doesn't," I said. "She came as backup last night in case anything went wrong when Bob and I showed you guys what we'd found. I wouldn't have asked her to come if I'd known how bad things would turn out."

He turned to Lucinda. "Is that right?"

She said, "Joe's my partner. I'm involved in what he's involved in. I know what he knows."

I said to her, "I wish you wouldn't do that."

"Too late," she said.

Finley turned to Monroe. "What else do you have?"

"What else do you need? Earl ripped you off. He ripped me off. The receipts and the reports tell you that. I can't tell you anything different."

Finley nodded and set his eyes on Johnson. "Earl?"

Johnson spoke softly. "That was very impressive. Total bullshit, but impressive."

"You can prove that?" Finley asked.

"Why should I? Like Bob said, I handpicked you guys. You trusted me when you joined me. You should trust me now when I tell you it's bullshit."

"You're going to have to do better than that, Earl," Finley said.

"And if I do? What happens if I show you that everything Bob and Joe and Joe's little friend have told you is shit?"

Finley shrugged. "Like Bob said, we all understood what would happen if any of us crossed the others. That applies to Bob and it applies to you."

Johnson turned to Monroe and said, "Are you good with that, Bob?"

Monroe didn't hesitate. He said, "I'm good."

Johnson turned back to Finley. "Go into my office. Look in the file cabinet—second drawer from the bottom. You'll find a folder of credit card receipts. Bring it to me."

Finley nodded to the man who stood behind me and he left the room.

For two or three minutes, we sat quiet. I felt calm, mostly. The records that Bill Gubman had given me would line up with times and dates when Johnson would have no alibi. Bill had made sure of that. Still, I wondered what Johnson was up to.

The man came into the room and handed a file folder to Johnson.

Johnson said, "Let's work from the present backward. Give me the dates of the reports and bank receipts in October."

Finley read the dates, then said, "If I remember, you weren't around that weekend. You said you were going out of town."

"And so I did," Johnson said. He dug through the folder until he found a receipt, which he passed to the man next to him. The man said, "Fuck," and handed it on. When Lucinda got it, her face flushed. When Monroe got it, his fell a little. He handed it to me. It was a Visa receipt for the Golden Crown Paradise Resort in Puerta Vallarta. The dates extended a day on either side of the records we'd given to the group. Johnson's signature was at the bottom.

When the receipt reached Finley, he asked Monroe, "How do you explain this?"

Monroe looked at me, and I said, "It's phony."

Johnson smiled and said, "These too?" He passed around a small stack of credit card receipts for Puerta Vallarta restaurants and a dive shop.

"Sure," I said. "They're phony too."

He shrugged and said to Finley, "I've got photos at home. If you want, I can get them or you can send someone else for them."

Instead of answering, Finley looked at his packet of photocopies and asked, "How about the nights of September twentieth and twenty-first?"

Johnson leafed though his file and shook his head. "I've got nothing for those nights."

Monroe smiled. I let the breath out of my chest.

"How about September fourth?"

Finley didn't bother with his file. "That was Labor Day weekend. We were together at your house in Wisconsin. You too, Bob."

I felt the room slipping away from me.

Finley looked shocked. He glanced at the photocopies. "August twenty-eighth?"

Johnson checked his file, grimaced, and thought for a moment. The grimace faded. "The previous weekend," he said. "I was training new guys in firearm protocols downstate. You can check at the department. The Travel Office will have the receipts."

Bill Gubman had said the dates on the receipts were good. He'd said Johnson wouldn't have an alibi. Something had gone badly wrong. Monroe looked scared. I figured I did too.

Finley said, "July thirtieth?"

Johnson pulled three more receipts from his file. "Out of town again," he said and handed the receipts to the man next to him. "Upper Peninsula Michigan."

Monroe shoved his chair away from the table. "Fuck this," he said and stood up.

Finley signaled to the men behind Johnson and me, and they grabbed Monroe before he could reach the door.

Finley said to Lucinda, "You want to tell us anything else about your Aunt Marta and her credit company job?"

"No," Lucinda said.

Finley nodded to two other guys. They got up and came to Lucinda and me. The one who came to me put a heavy hand on my arm. I shook it off and stood on my own. Johnson didn't look at us as the men marched Monroe, Lucinda, and me through the door at the back of the conference room. No one at the table did.

THIRTY

THEY LOCKED MONROE IN the same room as before. They put Lucinda and me together in the other room. The chair was still gone. Light from the hallway still shined through the hole in the wall. A blue blanket had been tossed in a corner.

I asked Lucinda, "Do you really have an Aunt Marta?"

"I did. She died of cancer twenty years ago."

"You shouldn't have done that. You could have walked out."

"It's done."

"Are you okay? Did they hurt you?"

She shook her head. "I'm okay."

Then she came to me and kissed me, like kissing me was all that could keep the world from crumbling at the middle and falling in on itself. I kissed her the same. My head spun. Lucinda clawed at the inside of my leg. I kissed her neck. She smelled like sweet, salty sweat. I breathed in and held her inside me. Her hand rose up my leg and she held me too.

I tried to say, "Stop."

"I don't care," she said. "I don't—"

A gunshot exploded. Small caliber—nothing to deafen you, nothing to make you want to call the police unless you stood nearby, kissing and groping for anything that could save you.

A heavy weight fell to the floor in the next room.

Another gunshot exploded.

Then nothing.

Lucinda let go of me. She walked to the wall by the crumpled blanket, leaned her back against it, and sank to the floor. She stared at the opposite wall, the wall that divided our room from the one where the men had put Monroe, the room with the gunshots. Then she looked at me. "You said Bill told you the dates were clean. Johnson wouldn't be able to talk his way out of them. What happened?"

"I don't know," I said, though I'd started thinking that maybe I did.

THIRTY-ONE

WE WAITED FOR THEM to come for us. We knew we were next. I wondered who would come. Finley? Johnson? Both?

Five minutes passed, and we heard the sound. The lock rattled and the door opened. Johnson stepped into the room alone, a 9 mm pistol in his hand.

But instead of shooting us where we stood, he gestured toward the door. "Come on," he said.

Lucinda pressed against the wall. I stood where I was. "No," I said.

"Don't be idiots," he said and stepped back into the hall, leaving the door open behind him.

Lucinda and I looked at each other for awhile. Then she got up and we followed Johnson into the hall. He stood by the door that led to the service elevator. He opened it, checked that no one was there, and waved at us to hurry.

"What are you doing?" I said.

"Trying to keep you from getting killed." Like it was obvious that a man who'd threatened us a dozen different ways would turn around and save us.

"Why?"

"Go!" he said.

"Why?"

"Don't you understand? We used you to make this work, that's all."

Lucinda said, "I don't get it."

Johnson shook his head, exasperated. "Will you get out of here before Finley and the others come?"

I asked, "Is Monroe dead?"

Johnson sighed and nodded like the fact saddened him. "Second shooting of an officer in two days. Both in the course of robberies. The coincidence will mean his death gets a lot of attention in the news, especially since he and Raj were friends."

I nodded, making slow sense of it.

"Now are you ready to go?" he asked.

I stepped through the door and Lucinda followed me.

Johnson looked relieved. "Take the elevator to the subbasement. There's a service door to the left. A van will be waiting for you."

"My car's in the garage," I said.

"Mine's down the street," said Lucinda.

"You've got a death wish? Take the van!"

"What will Finley and the others say when you tell them we're gone?"

"You escaped before. I'll tell them you got out again. Who's going to question me now?"

Lucinda and I ran to the elevator. Before it arrived, Johnson disappeared back behind the closed door.

We rode most of the way down in silence. Then, as we

passed the first-floor lobby and garage and dropped into the subbasement, Lucinda said, "What just happened?"

I could figure it only one way. "Bill Gubman set us up."

"Huh? Why?"

The elevator doors opened. To the right were rows of steel-mesh storage lockers. Pipes and bundles of electrical cables stretched across the ceiling. We ran to the left and I said, "He wanted Johnson to survive and Monroe to fall. That's not what he told me but it's what he wanted. We just boosted Johnson's power in the group. No one will challenge him now. And we got rid of his competition."

We reached the service door that Johnson had told us about.

"Why did Bill want that?"

I pushed the door open and cold afternoon air rushed in. A single flight of concrete steps went up to an alley. At the top, a van was waiting where Johnson said it would be. It was a police van equipped for handicapped access. Bill was in the driver's seat. He'd parked close to a Dumpster that was overflowing with empty cardboard boxes.

I said, "Let's ask him."

When Bill saw us, he pushed a button and a side panel slid open. Lucinda climbed into the backseat next to his folded wheelchair. I opened the front door and sat next to him.

"Welcome home," he said and turned the key in the ignition.

I reached for the key, cut the engine, and held the key away from him.

"Why did you set us up?" I said.

He held his hand for the key. "We really don't want to be sitting here."

I asked again, "Why did you set us up?"

He said, "The charges against you have been dropped. It

seems that the woman who thought she saw you at the construction site in Wisconsin has changed her mind. A case of mistaken identity. As for the Southshore shooting, our investigation has shown that you were in fact working as a private investigator, not as one of the thieves. The department will issue a formal apology to you—not something the superintendent likes to do, but considering the circumstances he agreed to it this time. It'll be on the news tonight and in the papers tomorrow."

He held his hand for the key again.

I said, "I was running scared last night. Peter Finley had locked me in a room but I got out. I'd gotten to a place where I was hiding and I called you because I needed help. I needed . . . I needed *you*. But you never called back. Why not?"

Bill dropped his hand and said nothing.

"Did you track my cell phone call to the house? Did you put Johnson's crew onto me there?"

Bill sighed. "Look, for this to work, we needed to play it—"

"Are Sanchia and her boys okay?" I said.

"They're fine," he said.

"If that's not true, Bill, I'll—"

He looked at me hard. "You'll what?"

I didn't answer. I hoped I would never have to.

He stared at me and seemed to make a decision. "When you got involved at the Southshore site, we already knew what Johnson's crew was doing. You could say, we were allowing it to happen. We'd pulled Johnson aside and made him an offer. He could go to jail for twenty years or he could help us. He's a bad cop but he's as smart and cool as you'll ever hope to find. We wanted him to infiltrate the city's street gangs as deep as he could go. We wanted names and addresses of every gang member. We wanted to know where everyone fit in the gang organizations."

Lucinda said, "So he's playing taxman to the gangs and collecting the information you want and money for himself."

Bill said, "It's brilliant. We'll know the organization of every gang in the city. Top to bottom."

"If it works," I said.

He said, "When you called in the burglary at Southshore, you just about messed everything up." He glanced nervously in the rearview mirror and out the front windshield like he thought Finley or other guys from Johnson's crew might be coming. He said, "At the same time, Bob Monroe was grumbling and talking about taking over leadership from Johnson. That would mess things up too. So we decided to use the first problem—you—to take care of the second problem."

I felt like Bill had punched me in the gut. "You did this without telling me or Lucinda?"

"I've seen you play cards. I thought we had a better chance of pulling this off if you didn't know." He almost grinned. I didn't. He said, "When the gangs find out that Johnson has eliminated Monroe, they'll wet their pants. And now Johnson comes out looking to the rest of his crew like he can do no wrong. We print up a few travel and restaurant receipts for him and he smells clean to them from now on."

Lucinda said, "He's really been doing solo burglaries?"

Bob nodded. "I told you, he's bad, but he's just bad enough that he can help us wipe out the gangs or most of them. No one wants to get in the way of that. Not the superintendent. Not the mayor."

I thought about what he was saying. "Not the FBI."

He nodded. "Not the FBI."

"They backed off when you told them?"

"They weren't happy about it but they did. In the spirit of cooperation."

"So what now?" I asked.

"Now we wait for Johnson to collect names and information. When he does, we make a sweep unlike any sweep you've ever seen. Maybe we'll even invite the FBI to the party."

"And what happens to me?"

"Like I said, your name's clear—with an apology."

"You think that'll clear my name?"

"It's the best we can do." He held his hand toward me again. "The key?"

"How about my detective's license?"

"Give it a couple of days," he said. "The department will present its findings about the Southshore shootings to the state board. The findings exonerate you. Sorry we can't turn you into a hero on this one, but there will be no basis for suspending your license. That'll have to be good enough."

I wondered if I wanted the license. I said, "I want one more thing." I gave him Rafael's name. "When you bring down the gangs," I said, "you're going to cut him free without making him agree to any deals."

"I can't promise."

"Can't or won't?"

"Won't."

I stared at him. "You used to be a friend, Bill."

His voice softened. "I still am."

I thought about hitting him. I thought about crying—for him, for me, for what we used to be.

I opened the van door and climbed out.

Lucinda slid open the side panel and got out too.

Her car was parked on the street. Mine was in the building garage. Getting to them seemed less of a risk than staying with Bill.

He yelled, "Give me the key!"

I held it so he could see it, then tossed it down the stairs that led to the basement. He could crawl down and get it himself. He could radio for help. He could sit in his van and wait for Finley to come and hold a gun to his head. I didn't care what he did but I wanted him to suffer.

THIRTY-TWO

THE GATE AGENT ANNOUNCED early boarding for the flight to Daytona. The morning was bright and cold. In the first light, before Jason and I got in my car to drive to the airport, the thermometer said the temperature was twenty-three degrees. The radio forecaster said clouds would blow in by early afternoon and an inch or two of snow would fall overnight. Still, a couple of jokers who were waiting for the flight already had changed into shorts, short-sleeved shirts, and flip-flops.

Jason came back from the floor-to-ceiling window where he'd been watching baggage handlers loading luggage into the bottom of the airplane. "Where is she?" he said.

"Don't worry, she'll be here."

He sat and ate the remainder of a sweet roll that we'd bought after clearing security. He'd knocked his infection and you would never know he'd been sick and in the hospital a week earlier except for the bright-red scar just above his belt where his doctors removed his appendix. When I'd taken him for his two-week postoperative checkup, Dr. Abassi had prodded the skin around the scar and told him that he still needed to take it easy.

Jason had said, "I'm eleven years old. It's impossible to take it easy."

The doctor had laughed and said to me, "Smart kid. You'd better keep an eye on him."

Jason shook his head like he knew more than the adults who surrounded him. "Joe needs someone to keep an eye on him more than I do."

"Smart kid," the doctor said again and left the room.

Now Jason ate his sweet roll like he'd never seen a hospital bed and never would, and he checked his watch and mumbled, "She'd better hurry up."

We all needed him to keep an eye on us.

AFTER LEAVING THE SPA Club in our separate cars, Lucinda and I had met in the parking lot at Belmont Harbor to figure out what to do next. The sun wouldn't go down for a couple of hours, but already on the eastern horizon the gray lake water merged with the gray sky like there was no difference between heaven and earth. The illusion seemed like a dirty trick.

For Lucinda's safety and mine, we'd agreed we should stay apart for awhile. She would bounce around from motel to motel and I would do the same. We would talk by phone. We would drive past our houses and the places where we usually spent time, and we would judge the danger hour to hour and day to day.

That first night, sitting on the slick bedspread of a cheap

Northside motel, I'd called Corrine. Last time I'd talked to her, she'd told me she didn't know if she loved me enough to stand by me with all my trouble.

Now she'd heard that the police had dropped the charges. She said, "I'm sorry that I said what I said." When I didn't reply, she said, "Will you forgive me?"

I said, "I never blamed you."

She said, "Can I see you tonight?"

"No," I said, "not yet."

"Oh," she said.

When I'd called after that, she'd sometimes answered her phone.

That first night, I'd slept hard and dreamless. In the morning, I bought the newspapers and went to breakfast. The department had issued its formal apology. News of it ran on the bottom of page six of the Local News section of the *Tribune* and page nine of the *Sun-Times*. Maybe a few readers saw it. No one would have missed the stories about the robbery and killing of the highly decorated Bob Monroe. Those stories ran on page one.

I'd driven around for the rest of the morning and stopped at Mom's house a little before lunch. Jason had gotten well enough to come home but for the same reasons that Lucinda and I kept apart, Mom and I decided he would stay where he was.

In the afternoon, I'd driven around some more. I'd called Rafael. He'd said Sanchia and her boys were okay but were thinking of moving back to Mexico to live with her parents. I didn't tell him that Johnson was setting up the city's street gangs for a sweep, but when he said that he planned to keep spitting at Johnson instead of giving him names and money, I told him I thought he was smart.

In the next few days, there was no more coverage of street gangs in the news than usual, but I didn't expect there to be. Bill's plan, if it worked, would take months, maybe a year. If the plan didn't work, the news would have more stories about cops killed during robbery attempts or when they crashed their cars into viaducts late at night with no one nearby to see what happened.

I slept, I ate, and I bounced around from motel to motel and stopped by my office and house from time to time. After four days, when no one from Johnson's crew showed up to kill me, I spent more and more time in the places where I lived and worked.

One night, a little after three in the morning, I woke in a sweat. I put on clothes and went outside and opened my car trunk. I got the sack with the Baggie of cocaine and the bottle of bourbon. Inside, I turned on the hot and the cold taps in the sink and poured out the whiskey. Then I opened the Baggie and tipped the white powder into the swirling water. Flushing it down the drain felt like burning money. It felt like pulling away in the middle of sex. I climbed back into bed and stared at the ceiling. I was still staring when the sun rose.

That morning, I decided to take Jason out of school for a few days and book a couple of rooms north of Daytona.

THE GATE AGENT ANNOUNCED a final boarding call. The waiting area was empty. We were supposed to be on the plane already, sitting in row thirty-one.

Jason eyed me like a parent who didn't want to disappoint his child and said, "She's not coming."

I twisted David Russo's ring on my finger. "She'll be here," I said.